XOXO I LOVE YOU

JULIE CAPULET

An epic love story

★ AN AMAZON TOP 100 BESTSELLER ★

A sizzling, addictive romance from Amazon bestselling author Julie Capulet

Lexi

Somehow I got an interview at Downtown, the "It" company of the decade. Of course I'd heard of the CEO, Rafe Black. His success story is legendary. He's elusive. Outrageously rich. Charismatic. Powerful beyond belief.

And, if rumors are to be believed, insanely hot.

None of it prepares me for what's about to happen. The unexpected connection. The all-consuming fire that ignites between us, taking over all rational thought and replacing it with pure, wild desire …

Rafe

I've constructed empires, dominated boardrooms and steered my fate with unyielding precision. But the minute *she* walks into my office, like something out of my wildest fantasies, Lexi spirals me into a maddening frenzy of need like I've never experienced.

I'm completely, dizzyingly addicted.

Lexi is the chaos I didn't know I craved. And now I'm powerless to resist her, no matter how much it costs us both ...

*This book is the first of a duet and ends in a cliffhanger. The second book, **XOXX I Love You More**, is now available.

****Note to Readers:** This is a super-steamy lust at first sight billionaire romance starring a completely obsessed hero. You've been warned :)

1

I STEP INTO THE ELEVATOR. And I do my best to ignore how seriously unlikely it is that I'll actually *get* the job I'm about to interview for. I have zero experience, since I only graduated about a month ago. My English degree from Stanford will (hopefully) help, and I graduated (sort of) near the top of my class. But this is *Downtown,* the "It" magazine of the decade. It isn't just a magazine, but a *scene,* with its own fashion label, lifestyle website, pop culture news blog and even a film production company.

My roommate came across the ad for CEO's assistant online only a few days ago. Given the glam factor, it almost seemed strange to stumble across it in a place like that. I would have expected Downtown to recruit from more exotic locations...like in Silicon Valley garages or on French Riviera yachts.

Anyway, I'd applied, and by some miracle, I actually

I

managed to get an interview. I knew every wannabe in California would be dying to get their résumés seen. Not because we have a lifelong dream to be a CEO's assistant, not at all. But because an underling job like this one might lead to other opportunities within the company—and it's a company every graduate on the planet would sell their teeth to work for. You knew that if you ended up working there, you'd not only rub shoulders with the rich and famous, but also maybe even *become* one of them. They were known for hiring young, hot, über-talented geniuses. Which kind of makes me wonder what *I'm* doing here, but I've decided to just go with it.

As much as I'd like to think I have half a chance, I also know it's definitely a long shot. The email informed me that I'd be meeting with an interview panel. I can picture it now: ten ultra-trendy, over-confident hipsters and one... me.

I take a deep breath.

At least I look the part. As I check out my look in the reflection of the mirrored elevator walls, I can't help but notice that my new makeover has definitely done wonders.

As soon as I arrived in L.A., my roommate Tess dragged me along on a two-day shopping spree and pampering frenzy. Tess runs a make-up and fashion blog that has around fifty thousand followers, so I figured I should probably take her advice. Now, I have a stylish new haircut. I've been massaged, waxed (and I mean *everything*), glossed and groomed to within an inch of my life.

New city, new priorities, according to Tess. *You're no longer a student, you're a hot young urban professional living the dream in the City of Angels.* I'd argued that I wasn't a professional until I actually *landed* a job, but she laughed that detail off as a technicality. *Looking like you do, it's only a matter of time. Employers love hot, and you, my sweet Lexi, are the total package.*

We're about to find out if she's right about any of the above.

I try to let Tess's enthusiasm rub off on me as I stare at my reflection. My long blond hair falls in sleek waves. Highlights of platinum catch the light. Those colorists really know their stuff. My eyelashes have been lengthened by some carefully-applied mascara, also by Tess. A light green silk wrap dress with a short, flouncy skirt hugs my curves and emphasizes the green of my eyes. I wondered if the dress was too fitted and the skirt too short for a job interview, but Tess ordered me to get real. *This is Downtown, honey. They work in bikinis half the time.* Which is true, apparently. She showed me an article about it. Their offices are cutting-edge, modern, ultra-hip and even have pools, swim-up cocktail bars, loungers and tread mill work desks.

To-die-for heeled Miu Miu sandals with feather detailing complete my outfit. The shoes cost a fortune even at seventy percent off, but Tess said I really need to up my fashion game if I want to be taken seriously. I begrudgingly admitted she's right. My wardrobe consists mostly of sweatshirts and jeans—the more comfortable the better, since I've spent the last four years studying 24/7, not to mention the years before that, which were much worse.

Tess also pointed out that my scary new credit card bill will spur my motivation to get earning as quickly as possible. I didn't bother telling her I have that motivation anyway, cringing every time I think of my gargantuan student loan.

Anyway, look out, Downtown, here I come.

The elevator pings and the doors slide open. I enter the lobby. It's all glass and chrome and is positively glimmering with bustle and excitement and glamor. A lone receptionist sits behind a tall desk with a massive print of the L.A. skyline mounted on the wall behind her. There's an etched glass wall next to it that gives a tantalizing glimpse behind the scenes: busy people and racks of designer clothing, desks and film promotion posters. Sliding doors are open, offering views of the pools and palm trees. Music is playing. Everything about it screams *YOU WANT TO WORK HERE.*

The receptionist watches me approach.

"Lexi Blondeau?"

"Yes, hi. I'm scheduled to meet with the interview panel at four thirty."

"Actually, Ms. Blondeau, something came up. You'll be meeting with Mr. Black himself."

Mr. Black.

According to Tess, Rafe Black is famous for his reclusiveness and also his ruthlessness when it comes to business. He's also rumored to be...ridiculously hot. Either way, I'm relieved. A one-on-one meeting sounds a lot less intimidating than a full-blown inquisition.

"He's expecting you," says the receptionist. "Go right on down this hallway. And take the elevator up to the 17th Floor."

The receptionist's phone rings and she points down the white marble hallway before she answers it. I want to ask her what number Mr. Black's office is, but she's already distracted. His door will probably have his name on it, I figure.

Fine, is what I'm thinking. *I can handle this. No problem.* Most likely, he'll be some aloof executive who will run through his list of questions, loftily mutter a we'll-call-you-if-we're-interested dismissal, then send me on my merry way. I already know it's a phone call that'll probably never come. I'll wait a few days before reality sets in, while I meanwhile scour the internet for something slightly more realistic.

I walk down the hallway, and press the button for the elevator. It might be a private elevator. It's not the same one that accesses the lobby of the building.

The elevator swooshes up in that ultra-slick, barely-noticeable way, which gives me vertigo. I reach the 17th floor in about three seconds flat. I teeter unsteadily into a hallway, which has floor to ceiling windows and a killer view of the hazy L.A. skyline, all the way out to the ocean. I take a few seconds to let my equilibrium settle more or less back into place.

So the 17th floor is the *top* floor. There are a couple of swanky leather chairs bathed in sunlight.

Everything is so *luxurious*.

I can't help thinking this would be a perfect place to sit and read a good book while appreciating the view. But of course I'm here for one reason only. To kowtow to the mysterious Rafe Black.

There's only one door. So Mr. Black is the *only* executive with an office on the 17th floor. Well, he *is* the CEO, after all. And the founder of Downtown. And now that I think about it, Tess might have mentioned that he owns at least part of the building. Or maybe the whole thing.

I knock on the door.

And I wait. I check my phone. 4:27.

It might be a full minute before the door opens.

He stands there, wide-legged, silhouetted by the sunlight streaming in from behind him. And—*whoa*—if I was expecting an ordinary, work-addled managerial type, I was sorely mistaken. *Hot* doesn't even begin to cover it. In fact, it takes a few seconds for my eyes to adjust to…just *how* gorgeous Rafe Black actually is.

He's tall, and big. His dark hair is thick and more unruly than you might expect from a CEO. He's wearing an extremely well-cut suit but doesn't seem entirely at ease in it, as though it constricts a barely-controlled wildness that's a definite part of his vibe.

"Mr. Black?" My question comes out breathy and cautious.

His eyes are a deep shade of dark, smoldering blue and have a glint in them that's kind of…electrifying. He assesses me, more than a little cockily. But there's an edge to him, and I get the feeling I've somehow caught him off-guard. He's more tan and rugged-looking than any businessman has a right to be. It wouldn't shock me if he spent most of his time sailing the Southern seas or wrangling bucking broncos in the hot sun. I don't know why I say that. He's got this outdoorsy look, which sort of clashes with the ultra-modern lines of his office and his building. He's too masculine to be called beautiful but it's a word that comes to mind. And it's the kind of over-the-top male beauty that'll hit you…*right there.*

Yikes.

As he opens the door in an invitation for me to enter, his eyes trail intently across my face and my body.

Wow.

This is already…*intense.*

"Ms. Blondeau." His voice is deep, tinged with bass notes that sound almost like a purr. "Please, come in."

I hesitate. Some deep instinct flickers. For a second I wonder if he might be dangerous.

My hesitation seems to amuse him, and he barely cocks his head and scalds me again with those smoky eyes, like he's challenging me. *I dare you.*

The brief, deep-rooted warning is overridden by something else. A curiosity. A pull that feels more complicated than mere attraction.

What I'm thinking is...*I don't care if he's dangerous.*

I can't quite tear my gaze away from his brawny shoulders and his burly arms, where the muscles are defined even under the layers of his clothing as he clutches the edge of the door with gripping, brutal fingers. As alone as we are, I can't help feeling like I'm walking into Rafe Black's lair. *No one will hear you if you call for help.*

I step into his office, and feel a small rush of anxious excitement as he closes the door firmly behind me. *Is it hot in here?* The automatic lock clicks into place. I can feel my heartbeat in strange places.

"You're very punctual, Ms. Blondeau. I like that."

A good start, maybe. "Please. Call me Lexi."

"Lexi." My name, spoken in that molasses-rich voice, sounds strangely erotic. Almost indecent. I find myself wondering what it would sound like...in the dark...as a growl or even a plea as I take his...

What the hell?

I force myself to focus on the reason I'm here: To. Inter-view. For. A. Job.

This is not like me at all. I'm a clean-cut girl, punctual, reliable to a fault. Socially awkward. And embarrassingly inexperienced. I have never in my life felt such an instant and desperate pull of white-hot lust.

Damn you, Tess! Why did I let her talk me into wearing such a short, clingy dress? I feel like my clothes are entirely sheer, like Rafe Black is somehow penetrating them with his predatory appraisal as he watches me.

"You found me without too much trouble?"

He's making small talk, to put me at ease, maybe, but I get the feeling that Mr. Black is perceptive, freakishly so, and that he's somehow able to read me very easily. Too easily.

Small talk isn't something I'm good at, but it comes more easily this time, for some reason. "Yes, well, I was glad there was only one door."

He smiles, revealing perfect white teeth.

Holy hell. He really is...very attractive.

"I bought this building specifically for this office," he says. "I prefer total privacy. I like the feeling of being removed from the rest of the world. What do you like, Lexi?"

So he does own the building. "Uh..." *Is he teasing me?* "We had to take personality tests in one of my psychology classes and the results said I'm ninety-three percent intro-vert. So, yes, I can relate."

"We have something in common, then." His eyes do that sparking thing again and...*oh, no...I'm blushing.* "No one can access this floor at any time without my permission."

"Oh." I already know I'm locked in here with him. That no one can get in and that I can't get out unless he *lets* me out. I also know that if I don't *un*lock my eyes from Rafe Black's sinfully perfect mouth right now, I'm going to do something I'll probably regret.

I find myself desperately hoping my reactions to him aren't somehow...*detectable.* My nipples might barely be visible through the thin silk of my dress, which has a sort of light, built-in bra that might not be fully up to its job. My skin feels warm and flushed, and I'm getting all hot and...*oh god...*

Flustered, I distract myself by taking in the surroundings. His office is huge. Three walls are windows and the fourth is black marble. There's the elevator and one other steel, space-age-looking door, with blinking electronic locks. A large desk sits in the middle of the room and there's a couch and several leather chairs. One of the glass panes has been folded open, and leads out to a huge patio area and a private pool. Tropical plants and palm trees decorate the space. Everything has clean lines and ultra-swish detailing. Clearly no expense has been spared. The design, at a guess, seems to suggest that Rafe Black is efficient, organized and...controlling. You get the feeling he does things his own way and will tolerate nothing less.

I walk over the window, looking out over the vast expanse of the city, which stretches out toward the distant strip of golden sand and the blue, blue ocean. "You have an amazing view." Okay, not the most ground-breaking observation, but I can congratulate myself on the blithe, offhand tone of my voice, even if it is slightly husked. At least I don't sound as shaken as I feel.

"Come, take a seat." He motions to one of the leather chairs.

I do, as he half-sits against his desk and folds his arms across his chest, causing his suit jacket to tighten against his arms. *Jesus, he's buff. He looks unbelievably...strong. If he wanted to, he could so easily overpower me.*

Lexi! I scold myself. *Get a grip right now, girl! He's interviewing you for a dream job, not "overpowering" you!*

I do my best to obey the little voice in my head because I'm still picturing him, *yes...holding me down...pinning me under all that big, hard weight...oh, hell.*

This is bad.

His mouth quirks in a languid half-smile, as though he's reading my thoughts.

Of course he can't. I just need to calm down, and now that I'm sitting, I do. I try to, at least.

But then he takes off his suit jacket and tosses it onto

his chair. *Jesus H. Christ.* The man is *ridiculously* built. Tall and muscular, but gracefully so, like a sculpture of a perfect male form. A perfectly *ripped* male form, with toned, hard muscles, as though he's spent the last six months sweatily lifting hay bales in the Outback of Australia or something. As my eyes kind of rove and drink in the sight—don't judge, this guy is seriously freaking hot—I can't help but notice, as much as I try not to, that Rafe Black is impressively built in...well...in *every* conceivable category. There's a sort of...very large...*gigantic, in fact...* *swell...*

Help me.

"Let's get started," he says.

Yes. Please. I need any distraction I can get at this point.

He reaches for a silver bucket on a stand I hadn't noticed before, behind his desk. He pulls a bottle of champagne out of its bucket of ice. "This might seem a little strange, but this bottle was delivered only a few minutes before you arrived. It's from my brother, Max."

"Oh. Are you celebrating something?"

"Today's my birthday."

"Happy birthday."

"Thank you," he says. "Can I tempt you?"

I can't even begin to describe how tempted I am. I know I probably shouldn't accept his offer. A glass of champagne will only annihilate my self-control, which at this point I badly need. But I can hardly say no. It's his *birthday.* "Thank you."

He smiles, and his gaze lingers on my mouth, before returning to my eyes. That brief, subtle glance has all the effect of a shot of pure, uncut aphrodisiac.

No one should be this good-looking. Or this much of a big, rugged, sexy tomcat. All I can think of is hot, sweaty, down-and-dirty sex—which I have absolutely zero experience with whatsoever—and it's freaking me out. I really have no idea what's come over me. "There's no reason we can't enjoy my brother's gift while we get down to business."

Rafe Black pours two glasses of champagne and hands one to me.

Then he sits in the chair that's next to mine. He looks even bigger this close. And even more manly and mouth-watering, if that's possible.

I could reach out and touch him...it would be that easy.
What would he do? Would he let me?

Somehow, I know he would.

His eyes blaze and I get that feeling again that he's able to read me—if not my thoughts, then...my vibes. With chemistry *this* off-charts, it wouldn't surprise me. I'm finding it a little hard to breathe with him this close to me.

"As you know," he says, "I'm looking for a new assistant. I've had the same assistant since I founded the company seven years ago. She's sort of a Moneypenny type. She's retiring."

"You must have been young when you founded Downtown, Mr. Black." I wonder if he's even thirty. He looks younger than that.

"Call me Rafe." His wicked mouth quirks. He's a rich, powerful mogul, obviously. And I'm an unemployed, entry-level nobody. I am, in more ways than one, at his mercy. His request for me to call him by his first name feels like...a small triumph. A connection. An invitation for familiarity that's ridiculously enticing.

"Rafe," I repeat. The name suits him. Strong, dark, commanding.

His eyes are intense, and I get the feeling that something about the way I've said his name has affected him. "I was twenty. Still at Stanford."

"I...also went to Stanford."

"I saw that on your résumé. It was one of the reasons I decided to interview you." I wonder what the other reasons are, but I hold my questions. Maybe it's best if he does the talking. My nerves have made me thirsty, and the champagne is the most delicious I've ever had. I sip again.

"Are you aware that Downtown is only one of the companies I own?" he says. "One of the smaller ones, in fact."

"I didn't know that."

"We run the magazine and all its off-shoots, as well as

several hedge funds, an investment company and a real estate brokerage firm."

I'm beginning to grasp just how rich and powerful Rafe Black actually is.

"I have to be honest," I tell him. "I've never been an assistant before. I did an internship last summer for a literary agency. The job mainly involved reading manuscripts and writing up reports. But I'm a quick learner and a hard worker. And very eager to please."

His eyes spangle, and I realize what that must have sounded like. *What's wrong with me? Why the hell did I just say that?* I blush again.

"I'm very glad to hear that," is his soft reply. "I think your résumé and references speak for themselves." His long fingers curl around the stem of his champagne glass. He looks like he could easily snap it without any effort at all. His eyes burn as he takes another sip. "I'm impressed."

I think I might be combusting inside this potent cloud of alpha-male pheromones he's emitting. My senses are hyper-aware, and my body feels unsettlingly warm...*and soft...and—oh, hell, this is way too much...*

Rafe rubs his hand across his jaw. He's so freaking... *sexy*...it's overwhelming me. His cinnamon skin, the stubble of his beard. *I can just tell it'll be rough and might even hurt a little.* His mouth, his thick hair, his dark blue eyes rimmed with thick black lashes. The man is an absolute specimen of hot sin and alpha male energy. And let's be clear about one thing: I'm not usually the type of girl who goes around thinking about alpha male energy *or* hot sin. Until now, apparently. "I do require that whoever I hire must be available immediately."

"I'm available whenever you want me." *Oops.* I realize the double entendre only *after* I make the comment, of course. Clearly my brain has turned to mush. My cheeks burn. "I meant, of course, that I'm available whenever you decide you'd, um, like me to start, *if* you want to hire me, that is."

"It's a demanding job. Long hours. I need someone who can basically be at my beck and call, at any hour of the day or night. We have affiliates in New York, London, Paris, Sydney, and so on, so we're a 24-hour business. It can be hard on…significant others, if you were to be working a lot."

"I don't have a significant other. I have a roommate, but she's busy most of the time, building her business."

"Good," he says, and his smug charisma hits me in the low pit of my stomach. God, he's so freaking cocky. *And it's doing things to me I can't even begin to describe.* "There will be times when you'll be required to travel with me. Frequently, in fact. Do you like to travel?"

"I haven't really had much opportunity to travel." I don't tell him that I never had the money. Or, that as a graduation present to myself, I decided to get my passport issued. Or, that it had just been delivered in the mail. Last week, in fact. "But I've always wanted to."

"Perfect." Rafe tops up our glasses. Then he reaches for a pen and a small piece of paper. He scrawls some numbers onto the paper and hands it to me. "This is the starting salary. Negotiable, of course. I'll cover all business-related expenses. You'll have a driver, and an expense account, if you agree to take the position. In addition, my apartment is in this building, and I have an adjoining studio apartment available for your use, if you have need of it from time to time, which you will, when I require you to work late."

I glance at the number he's written and hold back a gasp, wondering if my eyes are deceiving me. It's more than triple what I might have expected to earn from an assistant's job. A salary this generous will allow me to pay off my student loan within two years, especially if I can cut down on other expenses. Which I'll clearly be able to do, with all that he's offering me.

"What do you say, Lexi?"

"I say...yes. This is absolutely my dream job. Thank you so much, Mr.—"

"Rafe."

His black-satin voice seems to penetrate the air as a physical force, touching me and ruffling me. *How does he do that?* "Rafe."

He smiles. "It's settled, then."

This is happening so fast. I can't believe I just got *hired*. By *Downtown*. More specifically, by its drop-dead gorgeous CEO.

Rafe places his glass on the table and leans in his chair. As he moves, I catch a light whiff of his scent. He smells of soap and mint and raw masculinity. And there's more to it. Something elusive and outrageously, crazily appealing. The manly spice unfurls something in me, intoxicating me along with the champagne. My nerves are gone now, replaced by...sweet, soft, brimming heat. I feel reckless and a little crazy, if you really want to know.

My eyes rove down his long, powerful body and—*holy hell.* It's obvious that he's getting as worked up as I am. *His...the front of his pants...is straining...unbelievably...almost like it might...bust out...*

I can't handle this.

What would it feel *like?*

Lexi. Stop. Right now. Seriously. "When...w-would you like me to start?"

"How about right now?"

Our gazes meet. I'm having trouble breathing in enough air. I want to breath *his* air, his breath. That scent of him, that one hit, was not enough.

He leans closer. His dark eyes are burning with some unfathomable emotion.

Then, his hand lifts, brushing against an end strand of my hair.

He's touching me.

His fingers twirl around a soft lock of my hair, forming a lightly ensnaring hold. Very gently, he pulls.

I follow his pull. My self-control has been obliterated. I want this job, but even more, I want *him*. Sensing my consent, he pulls me closer, and closer, until my mouth is close to his. My nipples peak into tight little buds of sensation. Concentrated lust seemed to center there, and radiates slowly through my body in shimmery, uninhibited waves.

His lower lip is close to my mouth, as plump as ripe fruit. I'm high from his effect, and so desperate for more of that scent and the *taste* of him, I can't control it. This lust. This craving. It's bigger than me.

"Lexi." The whispered word is so dark, so deep. "I wasn't expecting—" He stops, his breathing heavier, as though he's conflicted.

I have no idea what's happening to me, but whatever it is, it's profound. I'm falling. That's the only way to describe it. I can't stop it. And I don't want to.

When his mouth brushes against my lips in a feather-light kiss that promises so much more, I touch my tongue to the rounded curve of his lip. He groans, and his fingers graze my nipple through the soft fabric of my dress. He teases it between his thumb and fingers, kneading it into a ripe bud. Searing sensation surges through my body.

Oh my god. This is really happening.

I gasp as he pinches tighter, rolling my aching flesh more insistently, controlling me entirely with his touch.

"*Lexi*," he says again, against my mouth. He cups my breast in his warm palm, squeezing lightly. "*Fuck*."

I get what he means. The ferocious urges of my body are driving me, and I realize with a tiny shred of concern that's swept away by an ocean of surrender that I'll do anything he asks. Anything. His effect is flooding me with fire.

He pulls at the knot of my dress, untying it. The fabric falls open to reveal my breasts. They feel full and soft. The rosy hue of my swollen nipples looks almost—and this isn't something I'd usually stop to consider—*sultry* against the pale white of my skin. I feel more beautiful than I've ever felt in my life. Because of him and the way he's looking at me. Like he wants to eat me alive.

Rafe makes a soft, savage sound. He seems overcome. He's torn, I can see, by the thought of taking advantage of me, his new, young assistant, if he'll even hire me now. It's a strange and sudden turn of events, and completely unexpected. But I'm too far gone to allow his internal dilemma to steal from me this stunningly needy anticipation. I don't care. I want him.

"Lexi. Do you want this?" His voice is low and deep and so appealing it pushes me past some barrier of self-control. "Tell me to stop and I will."

No. Don't stop. No stopping.

Very lightly, I brush my lips against his again. As soon as I do, his tongue sinks into my mouth, hungrily, filling my entire being with want. I suck on his tongue, gently greedy, desperate to take more of any part of his body into mine.

"*Lexi.* Fucking hell. You taste so damn good." His voice has become rasped with lust and...not indecision, but turmoil over a decision already made.

I want more from this beautiful, god-like *beast* than I've ever wanted anything in my life. He pulls me closer to him and I stand up. His gaze rakes sort of...*adoringly* over my body.

"You're so *beautiful*." He sounds awed. Just like that, like I'm already his, he pulls off my dress, so all I'm wearing is my panties and my heeled sandals.

I feel like I've just climbed out of some underwater seashell and been reborn as a lusty nymph who has no inhibitions, who's made purely of hot, wet physical sensation. I know the thin, clinging fabric of my panties is revealing to him...pretty much everything.

Rafe's dark eyes are heavy-lidded as he reaches slowly to slide his thumb across the saturated silk. I gasp because it feels *so good*. He licks his lips. "You're so wet for me, baby. I want to see you."

Rafe Black clearly isn't into second guessing things, because he rips my panties, with hardly any effort at all, tossing the tiny shred of fabric away.

This is happening. This is going *to happen.*

At the thought, I feel...happier than maybe I ever have in my life.

"Lexi. Jesus Christ. You're *unbelievably* fucking gorgeous."

A hint of shyness—some vanishing piece of my old self—loosens. I *want* him to see me. It's beyond crazy, but I want to entice him.

I'm standing between his knees. My breasts are close to his mouth. He takes them in his big, warm hands, plumping them to his mouth. Watching my eyes, he eases his hungry mouth around one of my nipples, licking and sucking in lusty pulls.

Oh my god.

I moan. It's too *good*, too rife with sensation. Each tug sends a wash of molten feeling deeper, lower. I feel unbearably hot and ripe, *there*, like I've been dipped in warm honey. I feel like I might...be close to the edge. Already.

His strong hands clamp onto my hips—*and holy hell, he's strong*—pulling me onto his lap, holding me exactly where he wants me. Our eyes lock in a connective link. A strand of his black hair has fallen over his forehead, somehow softening his severe beauty. I touch the thick silk of it, as our gazes hold, and a startling thread of tenderness passes between us, strengthening the lust, stoking it. "You're so damn sweet," he murmurs.

Tentatively, because I have never, ever done anything like this before, I ease my palm over the massive ridge of his hard-on. It's stunningly hard, and hot, even through the layer of his clothing. I try to unzip him, fumbling with the fastenings, too hazed in a trancelike eagerness. He helps me and I gasp when he's fully revealed to me. At the sheer size and perfection of him.

I touch him tenderly, taking his hot length in my hands, exploring and feathering with my fingertips. "*Oh, fuck,*" he groans. A bead of moisture seeps out of the tip of his cock. *Is he about to...?* I'm completely new at this and have no idea what to expect. I touch my fingers to him, swirling the wetness it until he's slippery.

Rafe's hand takes mine. "I'm going to come if you keep doing that, honey. Come here."

Rafe pulls me onto him and positions me so I'm straddling his hips. Then he begins to move me, closer, until—*oh god*—he's touching me. *There.* I let him move me along his length, until his cock is slick with my own juices. Rafe's thumb circles, centering, skating over the tiny nub, which feels electric and hyper-sensitive, igniting a sweet, slow swell. If he does that again, I'll lose it completely.

Instead, he guides the broad tip of his cock to my snug, slippery entrance, easing the head of his cock barely inside me. It's too much. *Feeling* him there. The pleasure is unbearable. My orgasm starts slowly. I'm riding some sort of precipice. My inner muscles flutter around him, drawing him deeper. "*Lexi. Oh, baby.*" Then he grasps my hips in a firm grip and, using the rhythm of my own body, pushes into me. I'm too tight, but the wetness and his thrusting drives force his thickness deeper. And deeper. His fingers glide over my clit, and the pleasure explodes in a rich, crazy rush. It feels excruciatingly good. I feel blinded with it. Needy and totally overcome. Each ripple of my orgasm pulls him deeper and we move together, grinding, needing more, until I'm fully impaled, riding the huge, thick length of him. His bold fingers work a soft rhythm, spinning my climax further, deeper, higher. Aware of nothing but the astounding pleasure, my body grips him tightly, and he groans like he's in pain. He's saying something but I can't comprehend it. *Wait. You're too beautiful. I can't hold on.* But my body is too possessive, too slippery. I'm riding him, pulling him deeper. I feel the flooding wetness, the thick, hot pulse of him deep inside me. The silky jets of his climax take me over another edge, the rush of spiraling waves milking him softly, again and again.

Oh.

Wow.

Just wow.

I'm floating.

I think I might be in love.

Is it possible to fall in love this fast?

With a complete and total stranger?

We stay there for a long time, rocked by the intensity of

what just happened. Of what's *still* happening. Rafe's burly arms are wrapped tightly around me. He's still deep inside me. My head rests on his hard chest. I can hear his heart beating.

I'm fully aware that, only a few short hours ago, I would have been shocked by my total abandon. I barely recognize myself. The consequence of what we've just done can—and probably will—be far-reaching, but I feel surprisingly removed from any of that. All I am is this moment. I feel supremely, ridiculously peaceful. I'm warm, and euphoric, cocooned in this haven high above the bustling city, wrapped in the arms and still wetly connected to a total (and unbelievably beautiful) stranger. I don't want to move. I don't want to break this bubble of bliss that, even now, holds on.

I don't know why I abandoned every sane, reasonable thought to get as close as possible to Rafe Black. All I know is that he's mine. I want to keep him. And I'll do it all over again if he'll let me.

It doesn't make sense, but that's just the way it is.

After a while, I move a little. With the small change in position, Rafe's barely-softened cock slides deeper inside me. I'm a little surprised that he's still as big—and *hard*— as he is. I have no experience with these things, but I think this might be kind of unusual. In a subtle adjustment, he moves me, causing his cock to swell even deeper in a vague, circular rub that triggers—*oh god*—a new, instant heat. I'm not sure how I can be so easily turned on—*again*—and so soon after what we've just done. He obviously feels the same way. He doesn't care about reason, just *this*. It's too powerful. *It's too insanely good.*

It seems amazing to me that he's still almost fully clothed. I want to get closer. I unbutton the top buttons of his shirt, breathing in his masculine scent, layered now with sweat and musk and lust. I touch my tongue to his skin. He's salty and mouth-watering.

"Kiss me," he says. "Give me your mouth."

I do, and he dips his tongue into me in a synced rhythm as he thrusts his big cock deeper.

He hugs me against his body, gripping me and easily lifting me. Still deep inside me, he lays me onto his desk. His messed-up hair frames his heart-breaking face. I *love* this: the cool, unapproachable top-floor CEO turned untamed, beefed-up sex god. His dark blue eyes glimmer and his gaze is tender under his lust. He kisses me again, like he can't get enough.

He grips me with both hands, lifting my hips higher so he can slide even deeper. It hurts a little. He's so freaking *big* and thick and *deep*. It's like he's fully occupying every-thing about me.

He slows his movements. He's listening to me, gauging every breath, every whimper. I'm not sure if I can come again, but his drives are measured and relentless. Rafe is reading my reactions as he plays my body, taking every quivering flutter to heart. With unequivocal insistence, he coaxes a rising surge. "Come for me, baby. I love the little sounds you make. Come for me, gorgeous Lexi. My gorgeous girl."

"*Rafe,*" I moan, as his thick length rubs against a ridiculously sensitive trigger inside me.

Cocky, he pushes the pleasure deeper. I ride the tidal wave, shattering. I dig my nails into his back, as my inner muscles work his own orgasm with long, tight, silky pulls. He doesn't try to pull out this time, and I don't ask him to. It hardly seems to matter. We're already bound.

You've totally lost your mind.

Yes. And there's not a damn thing I—or you—can do about it.

After the waves calm, Rafe strokes my hair for a while. He kisses my face. Then he pulls gently out of me. He stands above me, all hulking and outrageous. Then, abruptly, he pauses, touching his fingers to my body. He looks appalled, almost furious, as he stares at his blood-stained fingers.

"Lexi. My God. You're a *virgin*?"

2

RAFE

Fuck.

I can't believe I got so ridiculously carried away. *Christ. I just fucked my new assistant.*

The new assistant who's still peacefully sleeping in my bed with me.

I meant to pull out, at least. But I was so fucking overcome with lust that I spent myself inside her. More than once. There was simply no way in hell I could have disengaged myself from that tight little heaven on earth.

Goddamn it all to hell. That has never, ever happened before. Not even close. It didn't even *occur* to me to put on a condom. Or anything else. The minute that goddess walked into my office, with her sultry green eyes and her short skirt, practically oozing sexuality, my brain took flight and left the room. Leaving my goddamn cock in charge, which is never a good thing.

She's so fucking *young*, with a pronounced vibe of complete and total innocence.

The sane part of my mind wants to wake her, to politely ask her to leave, to tell her I still have a few more people to interview and I'll be in touch. I won't call. I'll send her some flowers and a gentlemanly note. Done and dusted. She's not the most qualified for the job anyway, not by a long shot.

I watch her as she sleeps, surprised at myself for even bringing her here. I never bring women to my apartment. It's a door I keep decisively closed. Until now, apparently.

Her sunny blond hair spills over the pillow in a silky cascade. Her pink lips are puffy from my greedy kisses, absurdly soft and tempting. The smooth skin of her jaw is reddened slightly from the stubble of my beard. I was rough with her. Too rough. I took her not only in my office —twice—but several times during the night, damning all consequences. And she's a fucking *virgin*.

Or at least she was. Yesterday.

She must be twenty-one at least. Maybe twenty-two. What kind of girl waits that long? And why?

Her dark-blond eyelashes lay in graceful curves against her pale cheeks, dark at the roots and lightening to an almost white-blond at the tips. Her make-up is all but gone, aside from some light smudges on the pillowcase. I think of waking her, just so I can see that sea-green burn in her eyes.

The sheet lays low on her hips, drawing a line across the concave plane of her stomach, framed by the jut of her angular hipbones. Her breasts are a work of art—there's no other way to describe them. Full and rounded, high and plush with youth. Her nipples are soft now, in sleep. And I can't resist. I'm already harder than I'd ever been. Maybe equal to yesterday, or last night. I hardly care about the comparison. What I care about is the soft bud of her rosy skin, tightening even as she sleeps, under the glide of my tongue. She tastes like nothing I've ever experienced. Sweet, somehow. Floral. Like she stepped out of a garden at midnight, while eating sugary cake and blossoming into full-blown womanhood. I suck on her like I'm trying to draw that taste from her body. It's perverse, almost, the greed and need I feel.

Little moans of pleasure come from her mouth. She writhes under the sheet, displacing it.

Fuck.

I'm a fucking goner. I'm whipped like nothing I've ever known. Just the sight of her is enough to blind me, once again, to every normal consideration. I've been a high-achieving, successful, responsible, Type-A paramour, sometimes more darkly than others, all my life. Every fucking second of my entire straight-A millionaire—actually, as of last month, *billionaire*—life.

But *this*. This *girl*. She disarms me. She makes me want to fuck everything up. I want to dirty myself, and her. Now

I know what it feels like to not care about anything but the moment, because *this* moment will be so good, so incomparably fucking good that nothing else matters.

I lick my way down her body, but I don't linger. I'm too frantic. Too needy. I let my tongue delve into her softness. Her willingness only compounds this overblown, excessive desire. Her hands are in my hair and she's lifting herself to my mouth, pulling me closer. I play her with my tongue, easing two fingers inside her. I wait for her to relax into the invasion. I know she's sore. I try to be gentle.

I wait for her to come to me, to beg for more. Gently, I zero in on the tender bud, licking and sucking her in soft pulls. Her moans and the clutch of her hands in my hair are driving me mad, but I remind myself who I am. A control freak. A successful, driven, disciplined man. A few soft moans of a willing woman should hardly undo me. But then it begins. Her hips sway in a back-and-forth rhythm. She cries out my name.

I'm mildly appalled with myself, with my reaction, how much I *love* that sound. Of her, calling to me. Saying my name in that dreamy exhale, like I'm some mythical god she can't believe. Like I'm too good to be true.

I'm about to come whether I'm inside her or not. And there's no question I'll take her, fuck her, make love to her. The semantics hardly matter. All I know is that there's nothing more sacred to me at this moment than being inside her. Her climax is starting. She's starting to spasm as

I slide my raging cock deep, driving into her and compounding her pleasure. If I cared about proving myself, of prolonging and lasting, the concern at that moment is inconsequential. That snug, pulsing embrace is so tight, so insistent, all my restraint is pulled from my body in silky, furtive tugs that leave me no choice. This is ecstasy in its purest form. The release is complete and total. I fall willingly, succumbing entirely to the perfect bliss of her, beautiful as sin, absolute as death.

It takes me a while to return to myself.

I can't think. I can only *feel.*

One thing I know: this is bad.

Very, very bad.

This girl.

I've found my weakness.

And I am utterly, hopelessly addicted.

3

I'M VAGUELY aware of a deeply pleasurable...fullness. I open my eyes.

Oh my god.

It all comes rushing back to me.

I spent the night in the bed of *Rafe Black*. Who's also my new boss (maybe). I'm no longer a virgin—to say the least. I got slightly drunk off two glasses of champagne at my job interview and had sex within thirty minutes (okay, maybe thirty-five) of meeting him. Very...*unprotected* sex. More than once.

And he's still inside me.

Wow.

It's a lot to process.

I start with the part about him...*still being inside me.* I'm sore, but he feels...good. More than good. *Insanely good.* That detail has already been well-established.

He's watching me.

His face. Stunningly gorgeous, candidly divine. Not perfect but somehow perfectly imperfect. I can see inflections of violet in his dark irises, which glow with a lusty playfulness that's quietly, shockingly endearing. I wondered before if it was possible to already be in love with him, and I wonder again now as we gaze into each other's eyes. His nose has been broken at some point. There's a tiny imperfection at the bridge and an almost-undetectable scar that somehow adds to his pirate vibe. His thick black hair is a glorious mess.

"Mornin', gorgeous."

"Hi." I almost feel shy, but it's a little late for that. He's not only seen but tasted, licked and penetrated practically every inch of me and is right now possessing me so completely he already feels like he's a part of me. Like if he pulled out it would break my heart.

His fingers are...*okay, wow*...ridiculously intimate. And...*oh...what he's doing with them feels very, very...oh god... good.* "Did you sleep a little?"

"A little. You?"

"Not really." Rafe kisses me, and the kiss is slow but full of passion. "I can't when the most beautiful woman I've ever seen is naked in my bed." His gigantic cock is very hard and he gives the hint of a thrust. I gasp. I'm sore but the pain is hot and pleasure-heavy. It's too much but at the same time not enough. "I'll be so careful with you," he murmurs. "I'm going to make you come again, baby. Then I'll make you breakfast and we can spend the day together."

Yes. Yes. How can anything feel as good as this?

We're lying side by side. My leg is hitched around his waist, where his hand grips my thigh. My breasts are pressed lightly against the broad, hair-roughened plane of his chest. Our heads rest on his ridiculously plush pillows as his mouth takes mine in greedy kisses. He eases me onto my back and pushes deeper into me, relentlessly, filling me.

It's more powerful than reason, whatever it is that's happening to me.

We haven't left his apartment. We've slept in blissful post-coital dozes. He fed me bites of chocolate. We showered once. And we've hardly disengaged. Throughout the entire night, hardly a minute has passed when his body was not somehow connected to some part of mine. The stroke of his tantalizing tongue. His clever, insistent mouth. The warm comfort of his big, hard body sliding over mine, thrusting into me, *so deliciously deep...*

With him, normal rules clearly don't apply. He's a drug, and I was hooked from the very first second I saw him.

If I'm addicted, Rafe seems almost crazed. Dirty and lusty and obsessed.

Like now. He's gripping me like his life depends on it, pushing the pleasure into me until I'm crying out.

It's too painful. I hold his face close to mine and kiss his lips gently as I wrap my legs around him more tightly, slowing his movements even as I take him deeper. "Shh," I whisper, calming him. "It's okay."

He's staring down at me, mesmerized. I can tell he's close. "Do you want me to stop?"

"No."

"Good. Because I couldn't even if I wanted to."

The pelt of his chest hair scrapes gently against my tender nipples. Everything he's doing to me right now is bringing tears to my eyes. The pleasure is pain-edged and brimming. It's happening. I kiss him. His hands squeeze me in lustful handfuls.

I arch up to him. The combination of his massive thickness, the delicious pain and the slippery friction is so beautiful I feel emotional about it. This power and this intimacy are *intense*. The curl of pleasure deep inside me reaches an excruciating peak, then breaks into shattering waves of bliss. My body clenches around him in tight, compressing squeezes as I suck gently on his tongue.

"Oh, Lexi. God, I can't take this." His words are slurred with his passion, with his effort to hold on.

"You can take it," I whisper. "Come for me, Rafey." I seriously don't know where this is coming from but I want to give him *more* and coax his pleasure and make him come as hard as it's possible to do. "I love how your big cock feels when you come inside me."

Rafe watches my mouth as I talk dirty to him. His eyes are lust-drowsed. He's looking at me like I'm some apparition he can't believe.

I've never even *thought* the words I'm saying to him, let alone spoken them. But this is the new me. Even though I'm completely new at this, when it comes to having sex with Rafe Black, weirdly, I feel like I'm...a natural. Already, I know exactly how to drive him and appreciate him and make him come like nobody's business.

I kiss him again, offering my mouth to him. Then I arch against him and squeeze around him each time he thrusts. The wet friction grows warmer as he plunges into the tight, silky constriction of my body again and again.

"Lexi. Oh god. Oh fuck."

A second wave of pleasure cascades in bright, tight ripples. Rafe groans as if his heart is being ripped out of his chest. His thick cock jerks inside me, flooding me with hot, liquid heat.

He collapses on top of me. His hand strokes my sweat-dampened hair. We're entwined and connected. It takes us a while to recover from the crazy intensity of our lovemaking.

"You're going to kill me," he murmurs against my neck.

We lay like that for a long time, just staring into each other's eyes as our bodies remain locked in rippling intimacy. Then he lays back, and the warm wetness as he pulls himself from my body makes me feel...sad. It's bizarre, but I already miss him.

He twirls a strand of my hair absent-mindedly. "Are we going to talk about the elephant in the room?"

At first I'm not sure what he means. "You mean your...?"

He laughs loudly. It's the first time I've heard him laugh and *I love the sound of his laughter.* "I'll take that as a compliment," he says, "but, no, I was actually talking about us having unprotected sex five times. No, wait. Six."

Oh. That.

"It was your first time, and I've never had sex without a condom before in my life, so we're probably good on issue number one."

I guess he's talking about...catching something.

"Do you mind if I ask you a very personal question?" His expression is relaxed, his eyes glinting.

"Since when do you ask first?"

He smiles wryly, until another laugh escapes him. *God, he's so gorgeous.* "I realize this is a question I should probably have asked you yesterday, right about the time you were climbing onto the biggest, baddest hard-on I've ever had in my life, and at my insistence."

I smile back at him, and my face feels warm. Yes, I did do that.

I have no regrets—now that I think about it, wild

horses probably couldn't have dragged me away—but I'm still amazed at my throw-all-caution-to-the-wind reaction to Rafe Black. Then again, as I drink in every detail of him, I know I'd do it all over again. Then and now. He's irresistible.

His mouth is curved in a sexy half-smile.

"Is that what you want to ask me? Why I didn't tell you it was my first time?"

"That's not the question I'm thinking of but now that you mention it, why are—*were*—you a virgin? You could have any man you want. Why did you wait?"

I don't answer him right away. It's a long story, and one buried so deep I'm usually able to convince myself it was only a long-ago dream. Or nightmare. Either way, there's no way I'm about to lay out all the dark details of my past. So I give him the short version. "None of the boys I met seemed...good enough." He's listening intently. "It just never felt like it was the right time." That's part of the reason, at least. Not quite the whole truth and nothing but the truth, but it hardly matters now.

He's smiling. "Amazing."

"What's amazing?"

"That you went through such a sudden, complete transformation the minute you walked into my office. That outfit you were wearing was something else, by the way. You definitely caught me off guard."

"I did?"

"After reading your résumé, I was expecting a mousy nerd in comfortable shoes."

I smile. "That *was* me, until only a few days ago. Painfully shy, wearing baggy clothes and thick glasses. And I was usually lugging around an oversized backpack. I have my roommate Tess to thank for my makeover."

He tucks a strand of my hair behind my ear. "No. No way. Even in a paper bag, you, my sweet Lexi, could never, ever be anything but stunning."

A dart of pleasure flickers in my stomach. *My sweet Lexi.* I love the way he says my name. I'm surprised, too, how much I also love the very personal pronoun he put in front of it.

"What's the question, then? What did you want to ask me?"

He kisses me again, like he can't help himself. "You wouldn't, by any chance, happen to be on the pill? Just out of curiosity?"

The way he asks the question isn't demanding, or dire, even though we might definitely have some very serious consequences on our hands. We have, in a fit of ridiculously intense mutual lust, thrown all caution to the wind. The small trace in him not only of humor but of shared, whatever-comes-of-it reality draws me to Rafe, in an emotional sense, more strongly than I want to admit.

We're in this together, is what he's saying. I haven't exactly been worrying about what comes next, but it's nice

—no, more than *nice*. It's ridiculously *connective* that he's taking this approach to our possibly life-changing recklessness. It would have been easy enough for him to usher me out the door with a polite goodbye kiss and a business card in my clenched fist, *just in case*. The fact that he shows not even the slightest interest in doing this is...it's caring. And honorable.

I wonder again...*is it possible to fall in love this fast?*

"No," I admit. "I'm not."

"All right," he says, not missing a beat. I love the sound of his voice, the deep chest-filling tone of it and the slightest rasped edge. "In that case, let me ask you another, even more personal question. If you don't mind."

"Shoot."

"When, do you think...you might be expecting to get your next period?"

Okay, this *is* personal. But, of course, he has every right to ask. We've just had unprotected sex...quite a few times. I remember thinking it, the second time he came inside me, right there on his desk. *We're already bound.* I don't know why I felt that way. Why it had seemed so immediate and so powerful. Or, why I haven't felt anxious, not even once, throughout the last...eighteen hours, about what might happen *tomorrow*. All I've been able to think about is now. Him. Pleasuring him with my body as he proceeds to blow my goddamn mind.

It's more than a little crazy. Who *acts* like that?

Rafe has many powerful effects on me, one of them being this: a silent and unfounded sense of reassurance. With him, I feel not only sexy, but also, inexplicably, *safe*. For no apparent reason except that he radiates a protectiveness I've felt from the get-go.

I wondered, that very first time I laid eyes on him, if he was dangerous. His dark eyes promised he would do *something* with all that burly strength, if given half an invitation. And I walked right into his lair/office, almost instantly deciding to invite everything he was willing to give.

Now, he's proving to me, maybe without even meaning to, that there's more to this than merely lust. A little glow of hope flutters in my chest, but I don't indulge it. I'm not sure if I even *want* to hope for any kind of future with Rafe. But I'm glad he's asking me these questions. He's sharing the responsibility, and owning it.

I think about his question. My cycle runs like clockwork. And my period isn't due for three more days. Nine o'clock on Tuesday morning. That's how precise my body clock is.

Today is Saturday.

Maybe in the back of my mind, I knew it was unlikely I'd get pregnant this late in my cycle. I wonder if different timing would have curbed my enthusiasm, as far as the past day's decisions (or lack thereof) have gone. Somehow, I kind of doubt it.

"Tuesday."

His expression doesn't change but he kisses me lightly. This time, I feel the effects of that kiss, not with my body, but with my heart. I'm not sure if I like the feeling or not. It makes me feel like my hunger has dug deeper. Like Rafe Black has penetrated me not only with his lust, but something more. Before I can begin to explore my feelings on that particular topic, he interrupts my train of thought. "Would you consider *going* on the pill?"

"I..." I contain a small flurry of happiness at the question. If he wants me to go on the pill, it's fairly safe to assume that he wants this whole...*thing* to last longer than one weekend. "I don't...well, I don't have health insurance at the moment. But I'm sure there's a free clinic I could go to–"

"You do have health insurance now," he says, gruffly, as though the topic annoys him. "It's part of the employment package. I'll get you an appointment for Monday, if that works for you. Then, if you're okay with it, you can start taking them immediately."

If you're okay with it. One thing I'm sure of: when it comes to Rafe, I'm *okay* with pretty much anything.

I already know he's a dominant type of person. He's the CEO of an entire empire, after all. He *has* to be dominating. He's used to calling the shots, and to giving orders. He's just succeeded in taking full control of my health, my birth control, my job, my accommodation and my sex life. In one fell swoop.

But the way he phrases it finds me agreeing. *If that works for you. If you're okay with it.* He's handing me the promise of money, safety, the career of my dreams *and* on-call multiple orgasms. But he's not assuming anything. He's giving me the choice.

It's almost like he's suggesting that *I* hold some measure of power in this relationship, too. Even if he's the giver of all these...*gifts*, there's more to this story. I bring out a vulnerability in Rafe, and I can feel it. I felt it when I took him into my body, and I feel it now, as he watches my eyes. He doesn't want to scare me away. He wants to lure me and hold me. He's grown attached to me, already, as I've grown attached to him. Strongly. He wants me *badly*, for now, to be with him and to stay with him. I can see it written on his face.

It makes me fall for him just a little bit more.

As if to prove me right, he says, "I'm supposed to meet my brother tonight for dinner at eight o'clock. I'd like you to come with me."

I'm kind of surprised. I know we've shared a surprisingly intense attraction. Our bodies are like magnets that can't resist each other's pull. But still. It seems too soon to be meeting his family.

"Thank you. But no. I should get going. My roommate probably thinks I've been abducted by aliens."

"You texted her," he says. I'd asked Rafe to get my bag

at one point late last night so I could text Tess. I knew she'd be worried.

"Yes, and now I should call her. Besides, I don't have anything to wear to dinner. I need to go home and change." I only brought one item of clothing with me, of course, and in fact I'm wondering where it might be located. Probably still tossed aside where we'd left it in Rafe's office. "I'm sure you and your brother have a lot to talk about. You catch up with him, and I'll go home and prepare myself for my new job. I'll see you on Monday." Even as I say it, I can't help wondering. Will he still want to hire me? Maybe I've blown the job interview by having sex with him six times. "If you still want me to."

He snakes his arms around my waist, halting my retreat. "It's still early," he says, ignoring everything I've just said. "Call your friend. Then I'll take you out to brunch. I'll take you shopping for some new outfits. Some evening clothes and some work clothes. That's also part of the employment package." We both know a clothing allowance is well beyond the scope of my job description. "Then we'll go to dinner. I want you to meet Max."

Some underlying emotion in his voice when he says his brother's name seems steeped with affection. I get the feeling Rafe and his brother are close. And I wonder why he wants me with him.

"Rafe—" I begin, but he pulls me back to him, mouthing my nipple, nuzzling and biting gently.

"Please," he whispers against my breast, biting more strongly. Holding me with his teeth and his gripping hands. His mouth gentles, drawing my sensitive nipple into the wet warmth of his mouth, sucking in tiny pulls. It's a strange sensation. Like he's feeding on me with a kind of tender adoration. He's worshipping my body, that's how it feels. Each little pull sends a wave of some indefinable pleasure into my body. Not lust, entirely. I'm over-satisfied, if anything. This sensation feels rare and vast and sacred.

It feels *real.*

What am I getting myself into?

What have I *already* gotten myself deeply, *deeply* into? With no thought or consideration, just feeling. Pure, unquestioned lust, with an edge. Like the lust was only the tip of a huge and invisible iceberg of emotion.

I let my fingers wander through his disheveled hair as he suckles me in this gentle, reverent way.

"I would like to go on the pill, yes," I tell him. "But I don't want you to take me shopping. I'll go home and then we can meet up later."

"Nope." He sucks on me again.

"What do you mean 'nope'? I just said—"

He bites my nipple gently with his teeth.

"*Ow,*" I push him away but he climbs on top of me and crushes me with his full weight. *He's already hard again?* "Rafe—"

"Those are the conditions of the job. I like my employees to be well dressed. Especially my assistant."

"What did your last assistant wear?"

"I never noticed. It's a new policy."

I glare up at him and try to wriggle out from under him but he pins me in place. He's so damn *big*. And so freaking *strong*.

"Lexi." His tone has the edge of a plea.

God, he's exasperating. He's so bossy. *And beautiful.* And persuasive. Maybe because he's used to getting his way.

"Please let me. I want to give you things. I want to make you happy."

Is this real? "I *am* happy, Rafe. You don't need to—"

"Then we'll go out and have dinner. You'll enjoy yourself, I promise."

He looks...hopeful. Like my decision will have a much deeper impact on him than it probably should. *We just met. Eighteen hours ago, he was a complete stranger. How is it possible that we're already this hooked and this...connected?* "I know I'll enjoy myself. It's not that."

"What is it, then?"

"It's so fast. All of this. Maybe we should take a little breather and—"

"Or maybe we should just go with it. Since it feels so good."

And what do you know, I find myself agreeing to his demands. "I guess we could."

He grins at me. "Good girl," he murmurs, as he starts kissing his way down my body.

"*Rafe*."

"Let me."

And even though I protest at first, Rafe—once again—gets his way.

His *mouth*, holy hell.

4

———

I'D NOTICED, of course, the outrageous luxury of Rafe's penthouse office and adjoining apartment. Real estate location aside, both are huge and fitted with wildly expensive appliances, furniture and decorations. I'm about to find out that going out on the town with him is taking Los Angeles to a whole new level.

A driver is waiting for us in a private parking garage connected to the building, with lots of extremely fancy-looking cars in it. I wonder if they're all his. Nothing would surprise me at this point.

Rafe tells the driver, "Take us to Rodeo Drive. We have an appointment."

Bossy much? Jeez. I guess it shouldn't surprise me that we're headed to the most expensive shopping area in the city.

I give him a look and he smirks at me, challenging me to protest. "I told you I wanted to buy you things. I'm about to buy you a lot of things."

"You really don't need to do that."

"I know I don't *need* to. I want to." He tips my chin up with his finger and kisses me lightly. "Please? For me? It would make me unbelievably happy."

He really is...kind of sweet. "I need my consultant to come help me decide."

"Consultant?"

"Tess. She's good at stuff like this. Shopping and so on."

Rafe laughs. "A woman who doesn't like shopping? You're definitely unique, sweetheart. I'll give you that."

I don't bother telling him that my experiences with shopping so far have involved begging, stealing and scavenging on what might be called an extreme budget.

"Call her. She can meet us there."

I'm glad he suggests it. Tess will bring a degree of... normality to this whole scenario. It's like I've landed in some kind of fairy tale. I need my bestie to make a cameo so I at least know I'm not dreaming. She picks up on the first ring. "What's going *on*, Lex? Are you okay?"

"Yes. Very okay," I confirm. "I need your help. Shopping spree, phase two, is about to launch."

"What? Where are you?"

"On my way to Rodeo Drive. Can you meet us there?"

Tess pauses for a split second. "Us?"

"Yeah. Us."

"That would be you and..."

"Um...my new...boss." At this, Rafe gives me a look that's half-devil and half-saint which makes me lose my train of thought because just he's so outrageously...*beautiful.* I've never met a person so stunning and it's a detail that takes some getting used to.

"Holy shit! Did you spend the *night* with him? You said you'd be staying at the offices but...are you—"

"Yes."

"*Lexi.* Are you okay, honey? Did you—"

"Yes." I don't want to have to explain, especially with Rafe eagle-eyeing me. "Can you come?"

"I'm going to kill myself ten times over, but no. I'm in Thousand Oaks with a make-up client. I'll be here for at least a few hours. She has some connections at Universal Studios, too, so we might meet up with some people after."

"Tess, that's fantastic."

"Yeah, it could be, if I can get some work for the studios. Are you coming back tonight?"

The way Rafe is watching me, playing with my fingers, I somehow doubt it. "I'm...not quite sure yet."

"I can't believe this, Lex. *Rafe Black.* Way to bag yourself a hot billionaire, girl."

I'm not sure if I've *bagged* anything, actually. At this

point, all I can barely handle is trying like hell to ride the roller coaster my life has suddenly become. "I'll call you later. Good luck with the meetings."

"Have fun, sweetie. Don't do anything I wouldn't do." She ends the call.

"She can't make it." Rafe must have been able to hear some of what Tess said. She *is* kind of loud, to be fair. "*I'll* be your consultant. I'll take good care of you." He seems to have this uncanny knack for sensing my unease and saying the exact thing I need to hear. "Trust me."

And here we are on Rodeo Drive.

We're met at one of the many boutiques by a personal stylist named Maude and led to an upper floor that has an open fitting room with views of Rodeo Drive. Plush chairs and four tall mirrors have been artfully arranged. We're served champagne. A team of assistants answer the stylist's orders for sizes and styles. Rafe takes a seat near the window, watching me.

"It's like Pretty Woman on steroids," I can't help but notice.

He smiles. "Except for one crucial detail."

I guess he's referring to the freaking *prostitute* detail, and the comparison is suddenly making me feel the tiniest bit uncomfortable.

"She needs an entire new wardrobe," Rafe tells the stylists. "Work outfits, evening wear, everything. Bathing suits, too. Resort wear. We have a trip coming up. And a nice coat for fall. Leather, maybe. Or suede. Something special. And shoes. And boots. Accessories, too. Whatever she wants. And we'd like to take a look at some jewelry."

And so I sip my champagne as Maude and her team dress me and undress me, outfitting me again and again. Rafe is checking his emails on his phone, making a few calls. He gives his approval from his perch, or he vetoes the selections he doesn't like.

Whatever she wants.

Two hours later, my wardrobe has easily quadrupled in volume, quantity-wise at least. Any one single garment Rafe has bought me is more expensive than the entire contents of my tiny closet in Tess's apartment.

At first I refused, of course, but Rafe wasn't interested in my refusals. "Let me. You're going to need clothes for work and for travel. We have a few trips planned." His phone rings.

I guess that's good news. He still wants me to be his assistant.

Before I can ask him where we might be going on our trips, Maude brings me the most outstandingly luxurious coat I have ever seen in my life. It's made of the softest suede, rimmed with fur. Once I put it on, feel like my newly-released inner goddess has found her regalia. This coat is totally *me*—if *me* could afford it, that is. It's perfect, and I feel perfect in it. I slide it on over the black silk halter mini-dress I'm wearing. Petite, sexy Jimmy Choos are held out for me to step into.

And my transformation is complete.

A girl could get used to this.

My worry is that, a little more than twenty-four hours ago, I hadn't even met Rafe Black. And now...I'm having a hard time picturing my life without him.

5

———

MAX BLACK LOOKS EERILY like his older brother, but he's got more of a bad-boy vibe and an artistic flair to his overall look. He has the same dark blue eyes as Rafe but his hair is a shade lighter: a dark sable brown instead of his brother's very-black locks. And his mouth quirks with the same contemplative pout.

But it's there that the similarities end.

After Rafe paid the bill for my shopping spree and sent all the new purchases back to his apartment—not *my* apartment, I noticed but didn't say anything—we made our way to the restaurant.

It's a clearly-expensive, dimly-lit Japanese restaurant. Max is already at our table, which is by the window in the corner, and raised. We have to take our shoes off and step up into the cushioned, cozy enclave.

On the drive to the restaurant, Rafe told me that Max

manages one of his investment companies for him, but that it's a relatively new appointment. Before that, Max had a string of jobs that "hadn't quite worked out."

As Rafe takes my coat and introduces me to his brother, Max kisses my hand, taking in the fit of my new dress. He must be a few years younger than Rafe. He's buffed-up, like his older brother, but has tattoos that are visible on his neck and arms. He has shadows under his eyes and a dark swagger that suggests he's seen a few of life's harder edges. There's a bruised vulnerability about him. Also like his brother, he's amazingly good-looking, but there's a looser, reckless edge to him. I can't help thinking that, while I'd waltzed into Rafe's private lair without so much as a backwards glance, I would have thought twice about entering Max's.

Despite this, he's likable. His smile is mischievous and contagious, and there's a playful glint in his eyes.

"Max, meet Lexi," says Rafe. "Lexi, this is Max, my much less handsome younger brother."

"I'm not quite as rich, either," says Max. "But I'm a lot more fun." He holds his lips to the back of my hand a fraction longer than he needs to. Still holding my hand, he helps me slide around the semi-circle velvet seat to sit next to him. Of course I don't tell him that the past twenty-four hours I've spent in his brother's company have not only been the most fun, but also the most adventurous, erotic and orgasmic of my life.

Max is watching my eyes as though he's reading my thoughts. I blush. *Damn it.*

"Behave," Rafe growls at him, sliding in next to me, so I'm seated between the two of them. Max already ordered sake and he pours three cups of it, to the brim. He hands one of the cups to me and I take a sip. It's warm and strong and delicious.

It's a luxurious feeling, to be hidden away in this lavish, intimate little booth between two big, handsome men. I'm dressed in a very-short black silk halter dress, a pair of la Perla panties, a pair of heels...and absolutely nothing else. My legs are bare. My shoulders and arms are bare.

I've never really felt beautiful, ever, before Rafe, but right now, I do. I feel young and fully *alive*, like I've just truly woken up for the first time in my life. My body has taken on a glowing, molten awareness. Rafe's hand rests casually on my thigh and the heat of it is already beginning to warm me with its promise.

Max's arm brushes up against mine as he reaches for his drink.

It's a new feeling. I've never been so aware of my own femininity. My newfound sexuality is sort of simmering within me. My breasts feel full and sensitive under the soft veil of silk. I can feel my pulse...*there.* The hem of my dress has ridden high up my thighs, partly because of Rafe's hand. This semi-aroused state of hyper-receptiveness is electrifying. I feel reckless.

I'm not attracted to Max Black—I'm entirely too overcome with the attractions of his brother. But there's an unspoken tension to his nearness, like a challenge.

My fingers twirl a long strand of my hair. All I can think about is what has just happened to me. Rafe...and the way his massive, thrusting cock felt inside me when he *came*, filling me with flooding warmth. *God.* My lips part. I'm getting wet and I wonder if they can *sense* that. I'm a little shocked at the crazy turn of my own thoughts.

Rafe's arm slides around my shoulders and his other hand still rests on my thigh. He's claiming me, almost unconsciously, and his closeness calms me. But I've never felt so...*wild* in my life.

What's happening to me?

It's him. *He's* the reason. Under the hint of mint and soap, there it is: his musk-spiced masculinity. God damn him, he's tantalizing. I realize it's the first time I've been out in public with Rafe, and I seriously hope I can control myself until we're alone again. I'm basically on the verge of jumping him right here and now...*of climbing on to his lap and writhing against him until I feel him harden...*

Lexi!

"So," says Max. "Where did you two meet?"

"At a job interview," I say, thankful for the distraction.

"Lexi is my new assistant," Rafe clarifies.

Max's eyes rove between my face and Rafe's. An easy, amused smile touches his lips. He takes in our postures, the way I'm practically sitting on Rafe's lap, and the way his fingers are resting under the high hem of my dress.

"Assistant?" Max drawls.

"Yes," Rafe answers curtly. "Assistant."

"*I* need a new assistant. Let Lexi come work for me."

"Find your own assistant," Rafe says. "Lexi's mine."

Lexi's mine.

Oh god, those provokingly possessive words do nothing to help my restraint. Against every impulse I'd ever had—before yesterday—I find myself *wanting* him to possess me. To own me. Desperately. *Right now.*

A waiter appears at our table. On second glance, he doesn't look like a waiter. He looks like a manager, or maybe the owner of the restaurant.

"Mr. Black," he half-bows to Rafe. "And Mr. Black." He repeats the motion again at Max. "Would you allow us to bring you an assortment of our finest delicacies this evening? As per the usual? What are the lady's preferences?"

The lady's preferences include raw meat but have nothing to do with sushi.

Holy hell. What's wrong *with me? I've become a raging nymphomaniac.* I force myself to pull my mind away from the recent memory of Rafe's glorious...*manhood. How hard it was. How good it feels when he comes in hot bursts.* The worst—or maybe the best—thing about my metamorphosis from nerd to nymphet is that I don't care. I want to get down and dirty with Rafe Black like I've never wanted anything in my life.

I realize right then—at an entirely inappropriate time and place—that I've taken him into my body many times and in a number of different positions, but I've never... licked him...there. *Or sucked on him.* Even though he's done that to me...quite a bit.

I want to. I wanted to take that big, perfect cock between my lips, to suck and lick and draw him deeper until he swears and groans in that agonized way he does.

Okay, I've totally lost it.

I force myself to focus.

The restaurant manager is waiting patiently for my answer, interpreting my silence as contemplation over the dinner menu selection. "Whatever the usual is, I'm sure it'll be perfect."

He bows slightly once again and walks away.

"The food here is good," Rafe tells me.

I don't mention I'm not used to Japanese food, or ethnic food of any kind. I don't tell them that I learned to cook for myself from a very young age, because I had to. There were many times when we'd gone without food altogether. I think of the night I'd eaten plain flour out of the bag with a spoon, huddled by the light of a dying fire as my mother slept with an almost-empty bottle of bourbon clutched in her arms. I was seven years old. That day, I decided to teach myself how to cook and bake and how to fend for myself. I made a vow to myself in that cold, flickering desperation that I would work and study until I could somehow hoist myself out of the dismal choices I'd been given. I didn't want to end up like her. Drunk and sad and alone. The very next day I asked my teacher for extra books, and extra homework. When the electricity bill didn't get paid, I read by candlelight. Little by little, I climbed my way out of that hole. I skipped a grade. I got into Stanford with a partial scholarship, and I escaped the confines of my dead-end home town.

The memory chills me by a degree, as it always tends to do.

I don't tell Rafe or Max that I'm not, actually, old enough to legally drink. Not quite.

Rafe and Max are talking business. I lean in to Rafe and let his warm presence settle around me. That delicious mint-laced spice of sexy masculinity.

I love the way he feels.

He glances at me. "Okay?" he says, like he can sense the change in me.

I smile. "Fine."

It's scaring me, how safe he makes me feel and how addicted to this feeling I'm already becoming.

We're having a good time, that's all. You can walk away and pick up right where you left off any time you want.

I hope that's true.

A part of me wonders if it would be best to leave him

now, before it gets too hard. Before separating myself from him will cause me to shatter into a million unrecoverable piece.

No modern woman wants *that* happening to them, and least of all me.

I'll give it another few days. Then I'll decide what to do.

6

———

RAFE

THIS IS nothing less than addiction, I know that. I'm fucking obsessed. I'm mired in some twisted, raging combination of the two.

I'm powerless to slow it or calm it. It burns in me like the hellfire that it is. I've always been prone to obsessive behavior. At least when it comes to work. But not women. At least not before Lexi. Always before, I maintained a comfortably noncommittal distance. I've dated many women, but always on my own terms. As soon as they became too needy or too demanding, I'd politely take my leave. I always made it clear that I'm not looking for long-term relationships. I've seen very few that worked. I don't aspire to that kind of forced restraint and no one has ever given me reason to feel or believe otherwise.

But *this*. This is something new. Something dangerous. What I need to do is focus. I need to get a fucking grip.

I can't even stand to physically separate myself from her. Pulling out of her, even after having one after another of the most powerful orgasms of my life, I feel a ridiculous but overwhelming need to *stay inside*. To never, ever leave that blissful state of connection to this soft, nubile girl whose every movement and every moan makes me want to occupy her and possess her and keep her all to myself.

But I'm a rational man. I have more discipline and control than anyone I know.

I can handle this.

I had to force myself to allow her to leave my bed. I had to physically restrain myself from demanding that she stay with me, behind closed doors, until I took her again, and again, to satisfy this savage, carnal beast that has taken up residence inside my body. It's not just my cock that wants her, although my cock has become permanently and painfully rock-fucking-hard from the minute she walked into my life.

I can't seem to *deflate*. And it's not just that. My entire *being* wants to drink her and eat her and feast on her unbearable beauty in every possible way. My hands want to feel all that creamy white skin, play in her silky hair, tease her cherry-pink nipples into taut little peaks. My mouth wants to fix itself onto every part of her, to delve into that sweet tightness that's so damn *responsive*.

She's like a nectar-moistened flower. Ludicrously enticing. As though she walked out of a fantasy and into my life.

And I, Rafe Black, billionaire CEO, am addicted. That's all there is to it. When she threatened to *leave*, to go back to her apartment for the night and see her friend, I felt a spearing jab of panic. Just the thought of her, vulnerable to any other man who might come along...it's unbearable. She'd be *out there*, without protection. People would *see* her. They might covet her like I do. They might try to entice her. To *touch* her. I simply can't understand how she's gone twenty-two years, or close to it, without ever being *touched*. I don't care what kind of makeover she was given. It simply doesn't make sense.

I practically begged her to stay.

I tried to roll over, to watch her walk out the door as I waited for the relief. Like I usually do. Usually, I savor that peaceful, slaked solitude that doesn't require pleasing anyone or putting up with insipid, overly-emotional demands.

Instead, my hands involuntarily gripped her hips. My mouth latched onto her as though to draw comfort from her, to drink in some kind of sexual-spiritual nourishment. *If you leave, I'll come after you*, I thought, and hated myself for my pathetic fixation.

Let her go. Clear you mind. You'll see her on Monday, I told myself, knowing I'd do no such thing.

What if she disappears? What if you can't find her? What if another man takes her and keeps her for himself?

Max is his usual offbeat charming self and it's a good

test. Of my own tolerance. I couldn't really cancel. There are things we needed to discuss. The investment company he's running is being audited and has had some issues with insider trading accusations that are still being followed up. I trust him, of course, even if his history isn't exactly squeaky clean. He's always had good instincts when it comes to business. In fact I've been surprised at how well he's doing with it. Max is rising to the challenge. I know he wants to please me and it's another reason I offered him the job. It was a way I could help him. And protect him.

I don't mind that Max is practically drooling. She's safe between us. He can look. He knows if he touches I'll beat him to a goddamn pulp. I can still kick his ass. He *wants* to touch, that's obvious. The girl is innocence and sexuality incarnate, all rolled up into one perfect package, so I almost can't blame him.

I manage to keep my cool, barely.

The way she leans into me like I'm some kind of safe haven only deepens my need to guard her and shield her. She's practically on my lap as we eat dinner and talk. It's all I can do not to roll her onto me and take her right there in this fucking little booth, Max or no Max.

My brother and I talk about what we need to talk about. He's meeting friends later to go to a club and a party.

Something about Lexi has fired up old memories and

as I'm talking to Max, I think about that long-ago night that changed everything. The look on his face. The blood. So much blood. It had been an extreme reaction, sure, but a justified one. And a very accurate hit. The guy had bled out right there all over our floor.

They'd taken Max away for over a year, locked him up in juvie where they dealt with delinquent, dangerous kids. They finally recognized that he'd acted in self-defense, and by then I was eighteen and could be his legal guardian. Those years had been a haze of hardship. Of fear. And anger. Max was such a little punk. What that kid needed was love. I don't know if he ever really got it.

Somehow, we survived. Some mixture of grit and desperation pulled us through. I'd been so driven to beat the odds that I just kept on going. I used work as a refuge. It was the only thing I knew how to do. I worked, and I protected my brother. The two threads are weaved into my soul.

Because of this, I have a sixth sense when it comes to sensing vulnerability, possibly.

And I sense it in Lexi. I'm beginning to realize that this is one of the things fueling my obsession. Aside from the fact that she's a nubile little nymph the likes of which I have never before seen or even imagined, she has the same underlying fragility as Max, and it rouses every instinct I possess. She fires up all the old urges that drove me to succeed in the first place.

We walk out of the restaurant together and Max kisses Lexi on the corner of her mouth. Some kind of volatility boils in me but I keep it under control. My brother catches my eye and laughs. Then he kisses Lexi once more, this time on her other cheek, more chastely, like he's aware that he might be on the receiving end of my fist if he pushes me too far.

"You've got my brother by the balls, Lexi," he tells her, highly amused. "And it's nice to meet you. See you next time." Then, to me, "Did you know there's some kind of get-together in the offices tomorrow night? The social club has organized a game night, Jenna said. Are you going?"

I vaguely remember the email. "We'll see."

"All right. Have a good night." He slaps me on the back.

With that, Max walks off into the night. He's a full-grown man now, of course, but there's still that small edge of disquiet as he walks away into the darkness.

The limo driver is already there, opening the door. He's a new one and I can't remember his name. As soon as we get in I tell him to cruise for a while and I close the tinted glass partition window.

Lexi is sitting all demurely beside me, not touching me. But she has this look in her smoky green eyes that's not even close to demure. She's been watching me watch Max. Like she's reading me, or attempting to. She's quiet, and has been for a while. And there's an edge to her. I've only known her for a little more than one day but I'm so attuned to her moods and her reactions, I noticed the change immediately. That darker, spooked side to her that makes me want to shield her from the world and everything that might cause her pain.

I lift her on to my lap. "You all right?"

She doesn't say anything, but kisses me once, slowly, lightly.

Her *lips*. Pink and glossy. A kind of rounded, youthful plumpness that women pay a fortune for but never come close to achieving. Lexi's lips are juicy and sweet, like she's just been licking on a virgin-turned-goddess-flavored lollipop. And they're opened slightly. Inviting me inside.

I slip my tongue into her mouth. She tastes so good I'm literally dizzy from the rush of lust I feel. I need more. To get deeper. She goes pliant in my arms in a way that drives me mad. Willing and deceptively submissive.

She moves a little, lifting, and I feel her hand on me.

Fuck.

Both her small, delicate hands. Fumbling like she's not sure what to do but doesn't quite care. She's unfastening my belt buckle, unzipping.

"I've been thinking about you." Her voice is a sultry purr. "I've been thinking about what I want to *do* to you."

I can't even answer.

I'm so fucking far gone.

She's gripping me lightly with her cool hands, playing

me. I can't bear how good it feels. "I've been thinking about how much I want to *taste* you," she's whispering.

Fuck fuck fuck.

She's shimmying down my body, her dress bunching. I can see the rounded curves of naked skin as she kneels down between my thighs. She's so small, so petite. Her strength is nothing compared to mine. Her strapless dress has fallen lower. She rubs her naked breasts along my cock, sliding her body over mine.

Ah, hell.

She's kissing me. She suckles on me like I'm a sugar-coated popsicle. I can barely handle it. The pleasure is astounding. The wet, tugging pulls of her mouth paint my cock with red-hot ecstasy. Each kiss compounds everything. Each languid stroke of her tongue.

I weave my fingers through her hair to keep her there, to feel her every movement. She's obviously inexperienced, struggling to find rhythm. It's this combined awkwardness and resolve that's about to undo me. Her fingers begin to explore, and her rosy lips ease around me as her tongue strokes me.

The release billows through me so forcefully I struggle to comprehend how it could happen suddenly and so jarringly. The bliss erupts in spooling, exuberant bursts. My whole body is coming. My cock jerks violently in her mouth and she doesn't pull back. Instead, she clamps her *teeth* lightly around me, so lightly that there's no pain except the pain of a rocketing orgasm so dire I don't care if I ever recover.

I'm hers. She's mine. That's all there is to it.

This girl *owns* me, plain and simple.

And there's not a damn thing I can do about it except hope like hell I can keep her.

7

"WE'RE GOING TO A PARTY, at the Downtown offices. The one Max mentioned. It's some kind of game night. It'll be a good way for you to meet everyone."

Last night I'd had the passing thought that maybe I should reconsider his job offer. It's far too late to separate the job and...*this*. Rafe himself. I wondered if I'm getting in too deep. I wonder if my wild new whirlwind romance with Rafe Black happens to be fierce enough to overwhelm, break and basically—if and when it ends, which these things tend to do—totally destroy me. I can feel that about it, already. It has a power that scares the hell out of me.

It also has the power to drive me wild with lust.

Today, I can go with it, I decide. Partly because I can't *not* go with it.

He's too damn...*hot*.

Rafe has a towel wrapped low around his waist. He's over by his dresser, taking something out of a drawer. The lines of his body are unbelievable. The corded neck. The perfectly-sculpted muscles and that light pelt of dark hair across his tanned chest. The veins that snake down the muscles of his arms. The flatness of his stomach. That V of muscles defined at his hips that are kind of fascinating to me. The arrow line of dark hair traveling south...*that I've licked.*

Wow.

His silky tone has already kick-started some kind of sweet churn inside me, like he's already *there,* touching me with his echo and his promise. As if he wasn't perfect enough, his eyes, as they glance over at me, are glowing with that crazy shade of deep sapphire that's almost violet.

"Sounds fun." I'm sitting on a chair by the window, drying my wet hair with a towel. I'll admit I'm a little nervous to be meeting the Downtown staff. They're always getting written about. How cool they are. How talented and innovative and glamorous. "I hope I'll...fit in."

"Of course you'll fit in, as much as the most stunning woman in the world is capable of 'fitting in' anywhere." He might be teasing me. "Besides, I'll be right there with you the whole time." And there he goes again with that *safety* detail. Which is, aside from his gorgeousness and his insistence on pleasing me at all times (okay, and also the fact that he can give me multiple orgasms at the drop of a hat), is one of the details I'm getting *too* addicted to, I know that.

I don't care.

Okay, I *do* care. But I can't seem to resist. He's basically the king of A-list alphas and even if my subconscious is screaming *this is too good to be true*, all the little strands of my DNA are sort of craving everything about him.

"Do you play poker?" he asks.

"No. Not at all. I've never learned how."

"I'll teach you. Or you can just hang out. People will be playing games, and swimming." He glances over at me. "But I don't know if I can handle seeing you in a bikini without being able to touch you. So I'm going to have to ask you to keep your clothes on, Ms. Blondeau, so I can at least attempt to control myself for an hour."

Ms. Blondeau. I guess he's referring to the fact that I'm his brand new assistant, about to meet his staff. It makes me wonder how all this will work.

Because I know what he means. I felt the same way at the restaurant with Max. It's going to be hard to not act on impulses *this* amped-up and out of control.

I watch him as he takes some things out of his drawer. The nearness of his big, sculpted, hair-dusted body is doing things to me. Weirdly, I feel like rubbing myself against him. Licking his skin.

"I have something for you. Actually two things." He's

holding whatever it is in each of his hands as he walks over and sits on the bed. "Come here."

I walk over to him. His black hair falls over his forehead in shiny ribbons and I touch a strand of it.

I sit next to him on the bed.

I'm naked under my towel and still wet from our shared shower.

"Hold out your hand."

I do, and he places one of the objects he's holding behind him before using both hands to strap a bracelet around my wrist.

"I bought this while you were trying on clothes yesterday. I asked them to show me some of their jewelry and I thought this one was sort of perfect. What do you think?"

It might be made of glass. The stones are too big to be diamonds. Something like that would cost an absolute fortune. Each glittering stone is encased in rose gold and hooked together to form a string. A tennis bracelet, I think they call them. Rafe fastens the bracelet so it circles my wrist.

"It fits," he says. "Do you like it?"

"It's beautiful. But you don't need—"

"I like buying you things. It's my new second-favorite thing to do."

"Thank you, Rafe." From my knees to my navel, my body feels hot and molten. The Rafe Effect, I've started calling it. "It's so...sparkly."

"Yes. Diamonds tend to be shiny." He grins at me. "That's one of the qualities they're best known for, in fact."

"Rafe. What do you mean? These can't be real."

"They can and they are, sweetheart. Now, let me give you my other gift. I figured I needed to...well, this gift might take a little more...adjusting to."

I'm still in shock from the realization that these many, many diamonds are *real* to fully take in what he's saying. "How much did this c—"

"Here," he interrupts, holding out his closed fist, which holds the second item. "Open it."

I begin to pry his fingers open.

Rafe smiles and opens his fist. He's holding two small, smooth silver balls connected by a short white cord.

"What is it?"

He places them in one of my hands. "Keep them in your hand so they get nice and warm. I'm going to get you very, very wet, baby. Then I'm going to put these inside you. As you walk around, as you move, they'll rub against an outrageously sensitive place inside you. You'll be on the verge of coming all night. You'll be so turned on that just one, single touch could set you off. It'll be deliciously torturous for you. You don't mind a little torture, do you, Lexi?"

"Rafe. No. I mean *yes*. I'm going to be meeting the Downtown staff for the first time. I don't want to be... distracted."

"It's only fair." His eyelashes cast shadows onto his cheekbones in the dusky lighting of his palatial bedroom. He blinks them innocently. "When *I* have to be so distracted." He pulls out the tuck of my towel, which falls to my hips. He touches one of my nipples with a single fingertip, drawing a light, rotating circle. "Have I told you how obsessed I am with you?" he says softly. "I think I have an unhealthy fixation." Rafe leans to lick my nipple. Gently, he sucks it into his mouth and plays it with his tongue.

I gasp. *God, I love how he makes me feel.*

His hand slides to my thigh and he eases my legs apart. His fingers slide intimately. "Do you know how much you torture me, sweetheart? Every single second. And tonight, it'll be so much worse. Because I'll have to wait. I'll have to see you with all those people who will watch you and talk to you and want things from you, and I won't be able to do this." He sucks on my nipple as he glides his thumb gently over my clit. "Or this." He eases his fingers inside me.

We just had steamy sex in the shower. I shouldn't be *this* turned on again, already. But I already know that whatever I *should* be is null and void when it comes to Rafe. He's my weakness. He already knows I'll give him anything he wants.

"I'm going to eat your luscious little pink pussy until it's soft and wet enough for me to insert these beads. But that's all you're getting for now. This time, you're going to wait."

I don't tell him, but I think he might be wrong about

that. I'm almost coming already, just from the soft glide of his fingers.

"Do it now," I breathe. I want him so badly, I don't care that I'm practically pleading. I can feel the very beginnings of my orgasm's rise, the adrenaline surge, the light quickening. "Put your mouth on me."

Rafe looks at me, his eyes narrowing. He removes his hand. He's seeing that he underestimated how turned on I am. He lays me back on the bed, running his hands over my skin, cupping my breast to take a nipple into his mouth. I moan from the feel of his teeth, scraping against the sensitive bud.

"Lexi wants more," he taunts. He pulls back. I feel his gaze on me like heat. I like the feel of that warm lust, centering on my vulnerable, soft nakedness. "You're a little minx, you know that? You want me to put these beads inside you now, don't you, Lexi?"

He lets his towel fall to the floor. He holds his thick, hard cock in one hand, stroking it in a languid rhythm. "I'm going to come. All over you. Right now. And tonight, I'm going to know, as you walk around, that my cum is all over your body. And that you're as desperate as I am. I'll know that all I have to do is to slip my hand under the table, under the short skirt you'll be wearing. All I'll have to do is brush my fingers against that *very* sensitive place, and you'll come, right there. You won't moan or cry out. You'll look into my eyes and I'll see the pleasure washing through you. And I'll know it's all for me. It'll be that easy." His breathing is heavier now, his eyes dark. "Do you want me to do that to you, baby? Do you?"

I reach for his cock. His hands slide over mine, allowing me to help him stroke his silky, engorged length. I squeeze him lightly. I tug gently on his cock, rubbing my hand back and forth in a coercive rhythm. Each time I move my hand forward, I try to pull him closer.

But he won't give it to me. He circles my wrists in his hands, like warm, living manacles. "You'll wait, like I tell you to." There's a teasing edge to his command, but also a stubbornness. He's not going to give in to me. "You'll come when I say so. Only then. And I'm going to make you wait for it tonight, sweet Lexi. So you know how torture feels." He pins my hands to the bed, kneeling down to breathe lightly on my hot, aching flesh, blowing little puffs of warm, caressing air.

"I *don't* torture you." I sound desperate and I am. It's not fair. "I give you everything you want."

Rafe laughs softly. "You torture me, sweet girl, like I'm walking a fine line between heaven and hell. Every second that I'm not inside you. Every second my mouth isn't tasting you. How will I not lose my fucking mind, having to *wait*?" As though overcome by the thought, he touches his mouth to me in a lusty, open-mouthed kiss. His mouth eats at me. His tongue delves, licking, then gliding against my clit. If he sucked me, I'd come instantly. But he knows this.

His licks are gentle and wet but he's doing this on purpose. He's avoiding rhythm.

He takes the round beads from my hand and carefully, one at a time, he pushes them inside me. I'm so wet they slide in easily enough, although they feel bigger than they looked. There's a full, not unpleasant ache inside me and my body clenches around the invading roundness. I lay still, letting my inner muscles adjust.

Rafe touches the broad end of his cock strongly against my hyper-sensitive nub, in a brief, gyrating press. The sensation is bright and intense, a bolt of promising pleasure that rocks me to my core. I begin to lightly pulse around the beads. But then, he pulls away before my rush can fully take hold.

"Rafe. *Please.*"

I want his big cock touching me, pressing against me, rubbing me and giving me the release I *need*. I writhe, wanting him to do it again but he's laughing. "You're getting so worked up, Lex. Relax."

"*Rafe. I need you.*"

"You'll have me. But not yet. Tonight, I'm in charge."

I'm in bed with the devil, that's all there is to it.

"Poor baby." He laughs, reading my desperation.

God. It's only getting worse. As I writhe, swiveling my hips in a sort of protesting plead, the beads, deep inside me, begin to roll. The fullness is indescribable, the pleasure deep and ruthless. Not enough, yet, to make me come, but I'm riding some kind of pre-orgasmic swell that feels maddeningly good.

Rafe slides his fist around his cock. I feel greedy and crazily aroused. *I* want to touch him. I want *my* hands on that big cock, squeezing and caressing.

"I'd fuck that perfect little mouth, honey, but I'm wary of the state you're in." He laughs again. He's so goddamn *smug*. I reach for him. With one hand I finger the smooth head of his cock, swirling my thumb across the moisture there. He swears under his breath. I let my other hand rove, playing gently, exploring. Boldly. I go further, wriggling my fingers, feathering, teasing.

"*Lexi*," he growls.

I press harder, working him with my hands. And harder. "Come on," I coo. "Come all over me. I want to feel your hot cum. I want you to rub it all over my naked body." Again, new territory for me, but this desperation he's driving me to is playing with my mind.

His too, apparently.

With a feral growl, Rafe explodes. He comes in pulsing, milky bursts that jet all over my breasts and my stomach. I love the feel of his pleasure raining over me, marking me as *his*. I feel owned by him, and coveted. I want all of it.

Rafe's teeth are clenched and his heavy-lidded eyes slightly bloodshot from the power of his release. He leans over me, bracing his arms on either side of me. He kisses me deeply, his tongue exploring in intimate thrusts, and there's a pronounced tenderness to his kiss that makes my heart beat faster.

"You," he says, his voice deep and hoarse, "are an angel with a taste for the devil."

I want him to keep kissing me, but he stands up and walks over to his closet. He pulls on a pair of jeans, leaving them unbuttoned.

He disappears into the bathroom for a few seconds and I can hear the water of the sink running. When he comes back, he's carrying a small towel. He sits next to me on the bed. "Let me clean you up a little. I've made a complete mess of you." I let him do what he wants. I watch him. If someone had asked me last week to describe my perfect man, I couldn't even have come up with something *this* beautiful. His jeans are open at the front. His cock isn't fully hard, but close enough.

I feel a little calmer now, like I've channeled some of his satisfaction, even though I'm still on fire. I lay quietly as he cleans me with the warm cloth. As he wipes the soft cloth across my skin, he kisses me. My shoulder, my throat, my breasts. He turns me over, and I can feel the beads' effect as a deep, swirling ache of pleasure. *Wow.* Rafe kisses a line down my shoulder blade, down my back to the curve of my hip. Then he leans in to kiss me in a *very* intimate place. I squirm but he holds me down. And then, to my intense shock, he licks his tongue into the puckered cove, pressing gently. His tongue sends a fiery, burrowing dart of need through my body, connecting the aching sweetness inside me with the place his tongue plays. It's a strange, debauched feeling and I squirm away from him. He allows this, turning me onto my back. "There," he says, laying the cloth aside. "Get dressed. We're going downstairs."

"No. I'm not ready."

"You're ready." His eyes are glinting, challenging me. There's that playful edge to him that's my new favorite thing in the world. He likes to bait me.

And torture me, apparently.

I try to gingerly stand up, as he watches me. The fullness inside me is insanely lush with sensation. I can walk normally, but each step I take washes me in a low tide of near-orgasmic pleasure. "I don't think I can stand this for —" *oh my god, I moved too fast* "—very long."

"You can stand it. Now we're even."

"I don't see how we possibly could be."

He licks his fingers. Then, slowly, as he watches my eyes, he touches his wet fingers across my clit in a brief, barely-there glide. "Because all I can think about is *this*." Then he stands and nips at my lower lip gently with his teeth. "And what I'm going to do to you later. Get dressed."

I feel...surly. Mad at him, almost. How can he expect me to *talk* to people like this? All I want to do is hold him down and rub myself all over him. *What's happening to me?* I've become a lust-crazed hedonist. "I can't."

He exhales a low laugh. "I'll help you, then." He takes

my hand and pulls me toward his palatial walk-in closet, where the new clothes he bought me are now hanging.

I follow his lead, mainly because I'm too dazed with lust to object. Each step is...kind of intense.

Rafe picks out a pink silk slip dress. He carefully eases it over my head, then zips it up the back. "Ready?"

"No," I tell him, and he smiles.

Bastard. I almost wish I wasn't so insanely...needy. For everything from him. For that smolder in his dark eyes to that arrogant smirk to the thick wave of his hair. I don't *want* to be this hooked.

But I am. And I've decided to wait until tomorrow to worry about it.

I go into the bathroom. I brush my hair and leave it down. And I put on some mascara and some pink lip gloss.

When I reach for some panties, Rafe takes them, his eyes mischievous and scolding. "No one will know but me," he purrs in my ear. "And if they leave the room, I might just have to reach under your dress and do this—" His fingers touch me again and, *oh god*, it's enough to *almost* get me there, but then he removes his hand and grins down at me.

I glare at him. I feel crazed. Reckless. "You're a sadist, you know that? And very twisted."

He laughs. "You have no idea."

And I realize he's right: this really *is* torture, not being able to touch him and take what I need from him, *when* I need it. Like right now.

Rafe's wearing a white polo shirt, which emphasizes his tan. His jeans are still unfastened. And his erection has gained momentum.

"I could..." I reach for him but he takes my hand in his.

"No, Lexi. Later, I said."

I'm pouting. "It's not fair."

"I'll make it up to you. I want you to suffer a little. Like I suffer."

"I *am* suffering."

"Not nearly as much as I am, I guarantee that."

I give him a look. He's *enjoying* this. But then, he clearly *is* tortured. His cock is hard again. And hot-looking. It looks sort of...painful. "Poor Rafey."

He pulls me up against him, cradling me against the hard pressure of him. "Fuck, baby, you turn me on something crazy." Reflexively, I begin to rock slightly, easing my aching body against him. If I can move in just the right way before he notices. If I can just find a casual rhythm before he suspects what I'm doing...

But he holds me still. "Lexi," he scolds me sternly. "I said no. Come on. It's time to go." He stuffs his oversized hard-on into his jeans.

Damn it!

I smooth my clothes into place and...well, I hope for

the best. Whatever "the best" might be. Coming while I'm sitting at the poker table? Or not coming?

Rafe pauses before he opens the door. "Don't forget who you belong to."

Something stands out about his comment, of course. He's talking about ownership. Instead of arguing with him about twenty-first century independence or gender equality, all I want to do, weirdly, is not only to agree with him, but to kneel down in front of him and take his raging hard-on into my mouth.

But he's pulling me out the door.

8

————

LEXI

THE DOWNTOWN OFFICES are crowded with Rafe's staff. I don't know much about employment law, but I wonder if it's even legal to *only* hire such young, beautiful people. Or maybe it's just the endorphin rush inspired by two solid days of back-to-back stellar orgasms. Maybe everyone just looks beautiful because I'm high on life.

Either way, Rafe keeps me close to him as he introduces one after another of the Downtown team, and he glowers slightly at their open-mouthed reaction to, well, to *me*. It might be because we're so obviously *together,* the way he has his arm slung tightly around me or the way his hand holds mine. Their all-powerful CEO is clearly behaving in a way that's new to them, you can just tell by the way they're staring at us.

I'm introduced to Eric, the senior executive editor of the magazine, who has blond hair and is dressed only in wet board shorts. If I wasn't so starry-eyed over the buff, outrageously hot beefcake who's become my new obsession, I might have thought the guy was reasonably good-looking. But my parameters have become a little skewed in the past few days.

Next, I'm introduced to Jenna, the senior editor of the lifestyle blog, who's got red hair and is outgoing and nice. She has a sparky intelligence that kind of wows you when you talk to her.

There's Cole and Josh, two of the software developers. They're probably only a few years older than me. They're sitting on stools around a high table, playing a round of poker with Max, who leans to kiss me on the cheek. "Glad you could make it," he says, winking at me before grinning widely at his brother.

Both Cole and Josh stare at me as I'm introduced, which seems to kind of piss off Rafe. I wasn't sure if he'd want all the Downtown staff to know that his new assistant is also...more than that, but this detail clearly isn't one that Rafe is worried about. He's, in one way or another, touching me the entire time.

I'm not used to this kind of a response from men. The staring. The once-over. In the past, I always wore loose, baggy clothing. I wore an outdated pair of glasses, because I couldn't afford to upgrade to something less nerdish, for reading, which basically meant all the time. The truth is, I dressed to deliberately hide my body. I didn't want to be noticed. I had things I desperately needed to accomplish so I didn't get stuck in a life that was too scary and depressing to consider. I *had* to get out. So I focused a hundred percent of my energy into academic achievement. Which also meant that I didn't really think about men or relationships or...sex.

At all.

A few guys asked me out in college, but I'd always been completely focused on getting through my intense work-load. I'd gone on exactly three dates, but each of these "relationships" always sputtered out before they really even began. I knew the murky secrets of my past made me wary, and prevented me from getting too close to people. To men, in particular. I knew why I'd hidden myself. And I knew why I never allowed anyone to get close to me.

Until Rafe. With bizarre and forceful clarity, he strode through my reservations like a rampaging bull. As though my childhood was as wholesome and idyllic as the ones I used to fantasize about. With him, I felt protected. I had no idea how he was able to comfort me in this way. It was almost like he'd opened some hidden door, releasing little pieces of myself I never even knew existed, then fed those appetites with lust and champagne and outrageously hot sex.

Now, the attention of these handsome men is flattering, and unusual. And Rafe's eagle-eyed awareness of it is reminding me of my secret...accessory.

I can feel the effects of the rounded beads inside me, gathering sensation. I'm literally riding some kind of pre-orgasmic rush. I know my cheeks are flushed. It's all I can do to act normally. I try to keep my cool, and ignore the fact that, if I happen to move in a particular way...*or if Rafe decides to ease his fingers under my dress...I might come at any minute.*

It's a crazy feeling.

I'm glad Rafe is holding my hand, and I wonder if he's having second thoughts about this whole evening. He seems tense and he keeps looking at me, like he's watching me for signs of...a meltdown.

When his grip loosens as he's forced to shake hands as his friends and employees talk to him and demand his attention, I disengage lightly, just *moving* in any subtle way I can to keep myself from going mad from the sweet heat that's slowly, slowly rising. Torturing me, as he promised it would.

As I walk, the beads roll inside me. They caress me from the inside. And they press strongly against every sensitive trigger I possess. The feeling is so full with pleasure I have to stop myself from moaning softly. It's maddening. I feel like my body is humming with a warm, electric glow, centering, pulsing warmly and radiating to the tips of my breasts.

I stand next to the poker table. The pool and its swim-up bar are nearby. There's a rowdy game of water volleyball going on and people are mingling and talking under the hazy lights of the warm night. I do my best to relax into my rising tide. Maybe I should excuse myself. I really do feel like I'm almost at a tipping point.

A waiter offers me a glass of champagne and I take it, wondering if I should. Will it make things worse?

I watch as Max plays his hand and wins the round. He stands up to talk to me. He's tall and sort of towers over me. I can see the edges of his tattoos on his muscled arms where his sleeves are rolled up. His dark hair is slightly longer than Rafe's, and curls over the edges of his collar.

"You in, Lexi?" says the guy called Cole. Eric sits down to join them. "Deal me in," he says.

"I'll just watch for now," I tell them.

Max turns his back to the other men. "How are you?" he asks me. "I'm surprised he let you out." He's teasing me, and he takes a sip of my champagne. I have no doubt Max Black is mischievous as hell. I'm not sure what to do with that mischief, especially right at this exact moment, when I'm on the verge of self-combusting.

Holy hell. I'm so close.

I see Rafe walking toward us. The open neck of his polo shirt hints at the light dusting of hair on his chest. His muscles are sort of straining at the pull of his shirt and as he moves closer, the look in his eyes as he approaches me is scorching and direct. Utterly possessive. He's so unbelievably sexy that I *know* that as soon as he touches me, it's going to happen.

I know.

Oh my god.

He snakes his arm around me, and his hand slides down the curve of my ass, where his fingers rove lower. I try to move away, because the press of his fingers is the trigger. I hold back a moan but I can't quite contain a breathy gasp.

Rafe glares down at me alertly. So does Max.

Rafe's eyes are dark. As dark as I've ever seen them. Narrowed. Reading something in my eyes and the flush of my cheeks. His gaze is knife-edged and savage. Sort of... *furious*, in fact.

And as I lean closer to him, holding his hand because I need to hold onto *something*, the flare intensifies.

The swell is rising.

Holy hell.

I move closer to Rafe. I want him to shield me from what's about to happen. There's nothing I can do to stop it now.

"Lex?" he says, his voice low, as I bury my face into his chest. I try to keep quiet but a low moan rises in my throat.

There's a chair next to a tropical plant and he sits, easing me onto his lap—which is a good thing because my legs aren't going to support me once this hits full-force, which it's already beginning to do. I can only hope people are drunk and distracted at this point.

The casual brush of his hand on my thigh as he watches my face. The hardness of his body. The roughness of his jeans and buttons and the hard ridge, pressing against my hot, aching flesh—it's too much.

And it's too late.

That infuriating warmth that promised to be so high and so good...it starts to throb. It rises, surges, hits a peak and then tumbles over it. I try to contain my reaction and I lean into Rafe's body as he wraps his arms around me, anchoring me. The world takes on a dazzling brilliance. The swell of pleasure inside my body clenches violently, the intensity unendurable. From my soft, pulsing core to my belly to my nipples, the pleasure rises in a mind-blowing swell. Ecstasy overflows, wringing through me in wave after wave of electric, raw bliss. I don't know how long it goes on for. All I can comprehend is how good it feels.

And then, when the waves finally die down into lush ripples, my awareness of my surroundings begins to return to me. Rafe's arms are wrapped around me as though to guard me.

"Wow," says one of the men, as though in awe. I can vaguely remember his name. Eric. All four of them are staring at me. Cole, Josh, Eric. And Max. Max gives Eric a look that communicates something very similar to *shut the fuck up.*

Oh. My. God.

I just came *in front of all these people. All these men.*

And they're still staring at me.

"Can you walk?" Rafe murmurs into my ear.

I stare, still dazed, into his eyes. I nod. I think I can.

"Lexi and I need to talk," Rafe says gruffly as he helps me through the crowd, into the offices and onto his private elevator, which slides closed behind us.

9

RAFE

As SOON AS the elevator doors close, she swoons a little and I scoop her into my arms. "You're in so much trouble," I tell her.

A small laugh escapes her, which only makes my already-rock-hard cock even more painfully fucking engorged. "It's your fault," she says.

"I *know* it's my fault. But that doesn't mean you're not in for it tonight."

"Do you think anyone...knew?"

I feel like punching the wall. "Only the four people who happened to be sitting at that table watching you."

The elevator door slides open and I carry her through my apartment and into my bedroom.

She's still laughing lightly, like my rage is hilarious to her. "Maybe they'll think I was just drunk or something. Or I fainted."

"Oh, don't worry, Lexi. They knew exactly what you were doing."

I carefully set her down on the bed. She's smiling, a little guiltily.

"You think this is *funny*?" I fume.

"It's a *little* funny. If I didn't laugh I'd probably go bury myself in a hole somewhere. The whole thing is more than a little mortifying."

"I'll go down there and diffuse the situation later. Max will be handling it."

"Handling it? How?"

"I don't know how!" I'm having trouble dealing with this. *How did I let that happen?* I'd completely underestimated how turned on she would get by those fucking beads. I'd played with fire and got more than scorched.

She came right there on my lap at the fucking poker table.

And they all *watched*. The lust I knew only too well was shining out of their eyes as they *heard* the little moans she makes when she's coming hard. Josh, the coding whiz. Cole, the guy I poached from a Midas touch gaming company to make our website more interactive. Eric, who's been with me for four years. I saw it in his eyes: he was coveting her, wanting her, listening and watching.

Well, they can't have her. She's mine.
Mine!

I'm furious with myself for allowing it to happen. I

should have known better. I shouldn't have put her in that position. I shouldn't have gotten her so worked up.

My innocent little Lexi.

The mere thought of my employees and their desire boils in my brain and infuses my whole body with a fanatical rush. I'm suffering from some variety of fury that ghosts along the fringes of my sanity.

Mine. MINE. MINE!

Even as I process my rage, I battle against it. I'm not a lunatic, last time I checked. I'm not one of those overly controlling assholes who dominates their women and lords over every move they make. That's not me. I'm the guy that gets accused of being too distant, too distracted, too noncommittal.

But now, as I pace and glare, I *know* I'm not behaving rationally. I *can't* behave rationally. I'm too fucking far gone. Even worse, I'm too fucking turned on. I'm too possessive of everything about her. I *need* her.

I placed her gently on the bed but my lightness was a wolf in sheep's clothing.

I go to my closet, where I keep a shelf of toys and whips and devices.

With most women, I get bored very easily. I take what I want then I leave them.

Until now.

Lexi's body is a drug I can't get enough of. I want *everything* of her. I don't just want to possess her, I want to *devour* her. I want to explore her and to own her and spend myself onto her and inside her in every possible way.

I want to make her *pay* for making herself so unbelievably fucking desirable. I'm going to use that desirability for my own pleasure.

I feel big and mean and resolute.

Her eyes are wide as I approach the bed. She's quiet and still, her only movement the rise and fall of her breasts as she breathes in an up-tempo rhythm. "What are you going to do?" she asks in her starry, almost-petulant voice. She's being sassy. She doesn't care that she just came in front of those men. She *wants* to torture me. She's fucking *enjoying* this.

"I'll show you exactly what I'm going to do." Roughly, I rip her dress, so her breasts are exposed. I rip it all the way off. Her green eyes are almost completely swallowed up by the black of her pupils. Am I scaring her? Good. This thought only feeds my need to dominate her completely. Her creamy thighs are parted slightly, so I can see the still-swollen lips of her flushed, bare pussy, glistening from the candied effects of her climax. The sight is enough to turn my hard-on, which already felt uncomfortably gargantuan, into a beast of pulsing agony.

"You're a naughty girl," I tell her.

Her response to this is to smile shyly. "It was your fault," she says again, all coquettish. Her insolence is making me crazy, not because I expect her to be obedient, but because I want to replace that impish little smirk with a mindless expression of pleasure-pain. I want her to suffer like I'm suffering.

I ease her thighs apart. I finger the lips of her pussy, slick and ludicrously inviting. I slide a finger into the hot hollow, astounded by how good she feels. Gently, I pull the string, removing the round beads. She squirms and gasps.

I strip off my clothes and I climb onto her, holding her in place. She's so small and feminine. She's easy to dominate, to hold in any position I want her in. And I'm in a controlling mood.

As horrific as it was witnessing my friends and my brother—which is even worse—watching her come, at least I can rejoice in the fact that I'm the only man who's ever been *here*. I feel a perverse pang of covetousness. I'll protect her with my life. I'll kill anyone who tries to get near her.

What the hell? Now I'm becoming not only a raving maniac but also a psycho.

And the worse thing is, I don't give a fuck.

I lean in to kiss the pillowy petals, licking into her body. She tastes like candy. I put my whole mouth on her, drawing her in, then pushing my tongue deeper into her. She makes a little moan of delight. But I'm not about to let her come again yet. Not until I'm coming right along with her. I'll make her as crazy for me as I am for her.

I lick her everywhere, readying her for me. I tease her

pussy with one hand and I glide my finger over the tight little cove of her ass, which causes her to squirm in a futile protest. I increased the pace and the pressure, and my manic wrath is gaining momentum.

"You wanted those other men, too, Lexi?" I growl, hardly recognizing the low, husky fury of my own voice. "Is that what you want? Like this?" I pushed my fingers a fraction deeper in a dual invasion.

She cries out and her hand grips my wrist.

The sound of her plangent cries brings me back to myself. I want to lace her pleasure with enough pain to intensify it. But I don't want to hurt her or scare her. I don't draw away but just hold her, allowing her to adjust to my forcefulness. I feel her relax a little at my stillness. Once she's gone pliant again, I swirl my fingers more gently, until she's wriggling along with me.

"I want *you*," she breathes. "No one else." Her voice is pleading. Which is exactly how I like it. I feel a masculine surge of satisfaction at her submission and her neediness. "Let me show you, Rafe."

She'll show me *when* and *how* I allow it: that's how this is going to play out. She can read my controlling state of mind, and she responds with a female tactic of her own.

She moves and sort of nuzzles against my monster erection, searching with her mouth, and I almost lose it right then and there.

It's too much.

She begins to suckle on me in docile, deferential little draws, kissing my cock, licking, then taking me deeper. And she's rocking her hips along to the exploration of my hands.

I'm going to come. Already. I decide to allow it. I know I'll be hard again soon enough. So I go with it. I let her suck the pleasure higher. I can feel the ecstasy gathering in a molten surge. I'm on the brink, coasting on a wave of hot, sweet certainty. I'm riding it. Her mouth clamps around my bursting cock, taking me deeper than she ever has. I'm coming in rolling, liquid throbs, down her throat, all over her mouth. It looks dirty, what I'm doing to her. Sexy-dirty and over the line. I'm hardly a boy scout but I've just come all over her face, for Christ sakes. In the most lusty, abandoned, I-don't-give-a-fuck-about-anything-except-coming-right-now kind of way.

It's not that I'm disrespecting her. Quite the opposite. I'm respecting her so goddamn much that I'm worshipping at her altar with the unrestrained fervor of the devout. She's the most religious experience I've ever had.

As though to prove this to her, I move to cradle her in my arms. I use the sheet to clean her face and I carefully brush the damp strands of hair back from her face.

That face. Seraphic and sweet. Eyes the color of light green sea glass. Her eyebrows are several shades darker than her hair and not plucked like most L.A. women, making her look young, somehow, and inexperienced. The friend must have overlooked the eyebrow waxing on the makeover to-do list, or maybe it's trendy again, who knows. I like the effect. The full, natural arch of her eyebrows gives her a small town look of naïveté and freshness: those traits that never fail to stir the protective urges in me. Small towns, in my experience, are to be avoided at all costs. Bad things happen in small towns. Children are vulnerable and darkness creeps even into the light.

I know Lexi is fresh to L.A. She not only told me this but it's clear enough from her look and her wide-eyed eagerness. She arrived only days ago, from Palo Alto, where she lived for four years. I've seen her résumé and I remember she came from somewhere in Oregon. I try to recall the name of the place and can't. Other than the forgotten name of some nondescript high school, where she excelled academically, a raft of achievements from Stanford, and a few summer internship details, I know almost nothing about her.

"Where did you come from?" I ask her, kissing her eyelids, the smooth surface of her rounded cheek, the corner of her sumptuous lips.

She seems to understand that I'm not really asking for specific details, that my question is more about wonder and gratitude over the fact that I'm with her in this moment and can't quite believe my luck. She doesn't answer me.

Once upon a time I might've been concerned about the

extent of my addiction. But now, I simply don't care about what I'm losing. If there's anything to lose, I'm willing.

I don't care if I've gone past some kind of self-imposed limit that says I can only *feel* so much. This is too intense. *This* pleasure is too captivating, just from that soft tongue teasing mine. I draw her tongue into my mouth, sucking it, and the sensation drills a white-lit channel of electric need straight to my cock, which rears up in a sudden, jolted swell. I'm instantly and miraculously rock-hard. Again. Already.

How does she do *that?*

Still kissing her, I lay her back onto the bed. Her body is supple and willing and easy to manipulate. I hold her down, bending her knees, opening her with my rigid shaft. The tightness of her astounds me, like pushing into a juicy, magical fist.

She gasps. "What about the poker?"

"Fuck the poker."

I hold her hips with my hands, forcing myself inside. She makes little moans and digs her fingertips into my shoulders. Tiny bites that might be the beginnings of a plea to slow down, to be careful.

In my mind I *am* slowing down and being careful but my body is speeding up. My need is a wounded bull in a sea of red flags.

Holding her in place and continuing the forceful rhythm until she's fully impaled, I reach for the vibrator.

Flicking it on with one finger, I glide it gently against her clit as my other hand explores. My fingers grip her backside, burrow between the rounded mounds of her ass, lightly pushing into the place I want them. I don't plan on pushing too far. She's new at all this. Two days ago she was a starry-eyed virgin. I already know I'm pushing her hard. I just hold the vibrator there, gently urging with slippery pressure as I thrust into her, sliding deep, again and again. I work an unrelenting rhythm so all sources of sensation converge into one. Incrementally, I increase the pace.

"Rafe," she whimpers. "Please." She doesn't know what she's pleading for. It's too much and not enough. And I can feel it coming. Her whole body is damp and writhing with surrender.

"Kiss me," I say. She seems to barely comprehend. She doesn't kiss me so much as offer her mouth to me. I slip my tongue into her.

She moans into my mouth as her pussy begins its voluptuous spasms, clenching so strongly around my cock, the pleasure is pulled from my body in gushing, seedy surges. Lexi's body is writhing as though to ease the excesses.

Her movement slows until she's limp and boneless underneath me.

I flick off the vibrator and toss it aside. I let her lay there for a while. She's completely spent, dazed and replete. I lift her and take her to the shower. I use the

European-style shower head to wash her, holding the pulsing jet carefully, intimately, to bring her to yet another dreamy rise. I dry her with a towel and carry her back to bed, holding her in my arms for a few minutes. Her eyes are closed, her face peaceful. Her head rests against my chest and I can feel the silk of her hair.

"Rafe?" she whispers.

"Right here, sweetheart."

I've never considered myself a deviant but my thoughts are sliding into crazy, crafty directions. I remind myself she's not only my lover but my employee. I could remove her from the distractions of this city for a while, to a place where she knows no one but me.

I want her to be entirely dependent on me for everything. I want her to *need* me. And I want to keep her all to myself.

I've already berated myself over my obsession. I decide I'm over being all conflicted about it. Fuck it. The extremity of it will probably pass soon enough. Then I can return to my blasé ways.

But even as I mull this thought over, I know it's bullshit. I can't imagine *not* being obsessed with Lexi. I don't *want* to not be obsessed with Lexi. Sure, the whole overblown scenario is enough to piss me off. But the only way through a problem is through it. So I decide to indulge my addiction until it begins to wear off, or at least until it begins to mellow by a single degree.

I detected the smallest edge of reservation in her tonight. I pushed her, maybe, just a little too far.

I'll make it up to her by lavishing her with tender affection and giving her everything she's ever dreamed of. I'll prove to her that I'm necessary. That she can't live without me.

I want to take her somewhere private, where no one else can see her, just me. Where she can be all mine and only mine.

Lexi has never travelled, she told me.

I'll take her to my estate in Kauai for a few days. Or a week. Or two.

When I'm sure she's deeply asleep, I tuck the blankets around her. Very, very softly, I kiss her mouth.

Finding my tossed clothes, I dress and shut the door firmly behind me. Then I make my way downstairs to smooth away any rough edges, to diffuse the situation, to make sure my employees and my brother—the loosest cannon I know—understand beyond a shadow of a doubt that Lexi is entirely, irrevocably mine.

10

"Hawaii." I've already said the word three times but can't seem to get my head around the reality.

"Yes," Rafe says. "It's a bunch of islands out in the middle of the Pacific Ocean where the water is as warm as the air. I think you'll like it."

"You have a house there?"

"Yes."

"How many houses do you have?"

"Six. This apartment, an apartment in New York, my house in Hawaii, an estate in Malibu, a bungalow in Key West and I own a small hotel in Paris."

Wow.

I might still be in a half-catatonic state from the intensity of what took place last night. I'd been taken in directions I had never, ever imagined. I'd not only had a ridiculously intense orgasm at the poker table as a bunch of strangers watched me, but I'd then been made love to so thoroughly that I was still reeling from the effects of the unbelievably earth-shattering triple whammy.

I feel like my soul has somehow been shattered and reassembled. The fit of the pieces is new and unpredictable, and I'm still adjusting.

It's true that Rafe opens doors in me that have never been opened, not just literally but figuratively. Each time he comes inside me, it seems he's filling me with himself, physically *and* spiritually. Like he's taking possession of me, redefining the chemistry of my body with his essence. I know what that sounds like, but it's true. He's changing me.

I've wanted him, each and every time. Voraciously. But there, as a tiny dark thread against a white field of longing and pleasure and satiation, is a barely-acknowledgeable sense of unease.

Possession.

Ownership.

Control.

There's no doubt Rafe has gained all of this and more. I'm his and I want to be his.

But I also want to be mine.

I can feel, at the outer edge of what's happening here, that I'm not entirely sure about the distinction. The power spectrum is unbalanced in some indefinable way. Money, probably, even though it's much more complicated than that.

I'm being swept away by him and I can feel that. But I have no idea how to slow it down or to even the scales. Or even if I want to.

I run my fingers over his chest, through the light dusting of hair, without even fully realizing what I'm doing. We're that comfortable with each other, that touching at this point feels normal, like we've already become an extension of each other.

The progression has been dizzyingly quick, to say the least.

On Friday morning, I was a hapless, untouched girl. Now, only three days later, I'm a fully awakened woman. With a rising, silky erection in one hand and a fistful of hundred dollar bills in the other.

What?

I have no idea why, but the entire bed—I just realize at that moment—is covered in money.

I sit up a little to take it all in. "What is this—"

"I won."

He must have gone back downstairs after I fell into my multiple orgasm-induced coma.

I blink at him. I can see that just that small movement, just the blink of my eyelashes and the curve of my lips, is mesmerizing to him. That he's unfathomably conquerable just like that.

This gives me some comfort. I'm losing myself in him. There are aspects of this headlong rush that are freaking me out. But I'm not the only one. He's equally overcome. I can read in his eyes that he's unsettled, too, by this tsunami of attraction. Maybe he's never had a weakness before.

He called someone at Downtown to tell them he wouldn't be in until later this afternoon. "When's the last time you took a day off?" I ask him.

"I've never taken a day off. Do you know how to surf?" he says, changing the subject.

"No." Of course I don't know how to surf. I almost mention how cold the ocean is in Oregon, but that would be sharing information that might invite more questions. I'm too practiced at keeping secrets to even go there.

And I can't quite absorb my new reality. *I'm going to Hawaii.* Never, ever in my life have I dared to dream for something so magical. I'm not just going to Hawaii. *I'm accompanying my sexy billionaire lover to Hawaii.*

Something occurs to me. "When are we leaving?"

"Tomorrow night."

I think about this. "Rafe?"

"Hmm?"

"I need to see Tess before we go." I'd texted her that first night and had called her the next day, to let her know I was okay. I'd been so...busy that I hadn't had a chance to check the messages on my phone since then. I knew there would be messages from her, demanding information. And it was fair enough. If the tables were turned, I'd be worried sick. "Today I'm going back to Tess's apartment for a while." I don't follow it up immediately but when Rafe's expression changes to one of almost stricken alarm, I add, "Okay?"

His mind is working on several levels, I can see this. "I'll come with you," he says, and his voice has taken on a darker tone. "And I'll take you shopping for anything else you need before we travel."

"You already took me shopping. I already have more than I've ever owned in my life."

He doesn't reply, but his hand moves to rest on my lower stomach.

"You don't have plans for today?" I say gently. "You don't have things you need to do before our trip?"

"I might." He's moody. His hand moves lower. "Would you prefer to go alone?" He uses his fingers in a lazy rhythm, reawakening the slow, intensifying burn. "You want me to leave you to it?" He increases the pressure, dipping two of his fingers inside me.

"Rafe." He must think of something other than sex occasionally, right? He really can't seem to get enough.

It's futile. He's rubbing my clit gently. I get wet and he uses the moisture of my arousal to swirl my pleasure higher. Until I'm slippery and willing. Until I can feel it coming.

But then he stops. He stares down at me, softly challenging me. "You didn't answer me."

By now my body is throbbing. "I don't like this game."

"What game?"

"The one where you tease me to get what you want."

"I like teasing you." He kisses my lips. "*And* getting what I want."

I try to roll away from him, but he won't let me. *Damn his super-human strength!* And damn his fingers...which are rubbing—*oh god*—a very sensitive place.

"Do you want to leave me for the day, to take care of whatever it is you need to take care of?" His mouth curls into a manly little pout that's kind of...adorable. His beauty, every now and then, has the power to stun me. "Or do you want me to come with you?"

I know he's testing me. No agreement, no orgasm.

I feel an inkling of concern at his tactics. I could protest, and stand my ground. But then again, do I really need to go back to Tess's apartment alone? What do I have to gain from spending five hours without him, when I know I'll spend the entire time counting the seconds until I see him again? What am I trying to prove?

He kisses a trail across my jawbone as his fingers continue their lazy rhythm. "Up to you, of course. If you want to spend the day with me, that would be fine. If not..." Here, he pauses his movement, teasing me yet again.

I want to challenge him at his own game.

"If not, you won't let me come, Rafey? Is that the game we're playing? Good thing I've already come a gazillion times in the past three days." I blink at him. "I can wait until later. Let me go."

I'm a little surprised when he actually does. He pulls his hand away and lays back onto the pillow, with his arm crooked behind his head. "Fine." He's pissed off. And there's something so...*cute* about his outrage. He's mad because he wants me with him. I can't really be too angry about that.

I can't help smiling at his expression. "You're mad at me?"

"I'm not *mad* at you, Lexi." As though my question is ridiculous.

"Then why are you sulking?"

His eyes are dark and as blue as stolen jewels. "I'm not *sulking*. I don't sulk."

"You are. You're sulking."

"I want to be with you, that's all. I want to take care of you and make you happy. I'm overwhelmed with lust, yes, but there's more to it for me than that. I'm falling for you. Hard. And I can't bear to let you walk out that door all alone, not knowing where you're going or if you're safe or who might be watching you. It's crazy, I know that. But that's how I feel."

My eyes start to sting, weirdly, like I might cry. I wasn't expecting him to say that.

I already know he's my weakness. What I didn't fully realize is that he's my freaking kryptonite. How does he know exactly how to soothe my deepest fears and at the same time stoke my wildest desires?

I touch a strand of his hair. I kiss his lips. I've already surrendered. "I do want you to take me. I want you with me. I want you to come with me everywhere I go."

Even before I finish speaking he's pushing his big cock into me, feeding my pleasure with the thick, skewering gift of his body. He's both gentle and fierce, stealthy yet aware, entirely focused on my pleasure, which only mirrors, triggers and defines his own. We come together, like we always do, and the pulse of our shared release bonds us just a little bit more.

11

Everything seems slightly off-kilter when Rafe's huge, shiny limo pulls up, with us in it, in front of Tess's pink apartment building, which looks just a little more unkempt than it did the last time I was here. It's like we've just flown in on our gleaming alien mothership.

Despite the searing intimacy of the past three days, I feel awkward when I ask him, "Do you want to come up?"

I can sense that Rafe is quietly curious—God knows why. Tess has been bursting with anticipation since I called to tell her *we* were coming to pick up a few things.

"Sure," he says casually. He's wearing jeans and a nondescript black shirt. Aside from the limo, he could almost be a normal, regular guy. If you didn't stare too closely at the watch, which is Swiss and might actually be solid gold. And the shoes. Even though they're basic and leather, they probably cost more than I've earned in my entire lifetime. Which, admittedly, isn't all that much. (Oh, and the tiny detail that he's without a doubt the sexiest man I've ever seen or even imagined.)

The driver opens the door for me and I thank him and climb out. Rafe follows. It feels weird, to be standing in this place that's familiar but also now entirely changed. Rafe is like a giant sun, casting his tall, magnificent light onto the dingy and the mundane, recasting the world and my life with his brilliance. As much as I might have questioned my decision to invite him, I find that I *like* having him here with me. Of course I do. He's gorgeous and out of place and smiling at me like he's fully in the moment, as strange as this moment might be. And I love him for that.

Love.

Noooo. I backtrack. I find his accepting, I'm-with-you vibe...sweet. That's about as much as I can handle admitting to myself. *I'm falling for you. Hard.* What could I say to that? *I'm falling hard for you, too, Rafe. If I knew how to love, that is—which I don't. I'm too damaged, maybe. My heart resides in a cage and that key got tossed into the abyss a long time ago.* "This is it."

"Pink," he observes, very correctly.

"Yes."

He crooks his arm. "Shall we?"

I link my arm through his. We walk past the wall of pink (keeping with the theme) wall of metal mailboxes. I hadn't even gotten around to adding my name to Tess's mailbox, and as we walk past them I wonder if I ever will. The realization that this, now, might never happen is...in equal parts scary...and also hopeful.

The elevator takes us to the third floor. It creaks, rumbles to a stop, then—after a few seconds of wondering if we might actually be trapped in here—it slides open. The door to 3F is, unsurprisingly, wide open and filled with the excitable vision of Tess, who's dressed to the nines, in a red sundress with white polka dots. She's wearing her signature siren-red lipstick. Not only because a hot billionaire is visiting 3F, but because that's just Tess.

She looks adorable, as always.

Tess's eyes widen when she sees Rafe and she is, very uncharacteristically, momentarily speechless.

"Tess, meet Rafe. Rafe, my best friend, Tess."

Rafe takes her hand and plants a kiss on the back of her knuckles in an old-fashioned, gentlemanly kind of way. Tess is positively gushing with excitement. "It's *so* nice to meet you. I couldn't believe it when Lexi told me *Rafe Black* was coming with her!"

Tess ushers us into the tiny apartment, which is as clean as it can get. Still, after the opulence of Rafe's place, it looks different than it did three days ago. I'm not sure what to think about that. Extreme opulence, I'm finding, for better or worse, is very easy to adjust to.

Tess freezes as she notices my boots, one of three pairs

Rafe bought me during our shopping spree on Rodeo Drive. "Holy shit, Lex. Are those *Balenciaga*?"

"Um...yeah. I think they are."

"Do you know much those—?" She catches herself, and glances at Rafe. "I mean, they're...well, I saw them online and...they're a limited edition, that's all."

Tess touches the fabric of my dress, a thin film of blue silk that hugs my body like a second skin. She shakes her head and laughs a little. "Well, I have to say it. My makeover barely scratched the surface. Rafe's, on the other hand, has completely transformed you."

I smile back at her, a little embarrassed, thinking to myself that her comment might be the understatement of the millennium. I feel like an entirely different person to the half-dressed, virginal waif who'd bumbled my way to a random job interview last Friday.

"We can't stay long," I tell her, suddenly feeling unusually confined in the tiny room. "I've just come to pick up a few of my things." I'm not sure how to bring this up casually so I just say it: "We're leaving for Hawaii tomorrow night."

Tess's mouth drops open. She stares at me, then at Rafe, who's sitting on the second-hand blue couch, looking like a Greek god who's decided to slum it with the mortals for the afternoon just to see what mundanity feels like for an hour or two.

And just like that, I don't feel like there's anything in

this apartment I actually need. I don't need—or want—any of my old clothes anymore. Why had I been thinking my bulky canvas duffel bag was something I might use?

I don't want any of it. What I want to do is to give Tess a huge hug, arrange to see her when I get back, and then leave.

"Will you join us for lunch?" Rafe asks Tess.

Tess and I have been friends since we were freshmen at Stanford. We struck up a friendship in an American literature class. She's bubbly and fun and she brought me out of my shell, at least a little. Of course I didn't tell her *everything*. Some secrets are just too deeply buried. But I've shared more of my life story with Tess than with anyone I've ever known. She's been a light relief against the dark chasm of my past and my dogged focus on achieving against all odds.

I feel a little guilty for the flicker of relief when she says, "I would *so* love to come with you two! But I can't. I have a work thing. I'm getting sponsorship from a big name beauty products company. It could be my big break so I can't really cancel. I have to kiss ass and do as I'm told. That's what it takes to get ahead...you know what it's like." She falters. We both might be thinking the same thing.

Tess is too kind-hearted to intend anything callous or mean-spirited. But something about the reality of the situation digs deep. The Pretty Woman One Step Removed scenario.

Is *that* what I'm doing? Kissing his ass and sucking his cock so I can wear Balenciaga boots and land my dream job and go to Hawaii?

No. Of course it's not like that. It's nothing like that.

The perks of my new arrangement are too many to list, too life-changing to analyze. But the fact is, I want to distance myself from this shabby little apartment and my depressing history to...if not ride into the sunset with Rafe, at least to...go with it. For now. To see where it takes us.

It's confusing to want more than you might be able to handle.

I walk over to Tess and give her a big hug. "Good luck with the sponsors. I'll call you in a few days."

She hugs me right back. Both of us have tears in our eyes as we draw apart. I don't think either of us even know what we're crying about except that we can both feel it: a change. In me. "Did you get everything you need?"

"I decided I don't really need anything," I tell her. "I just wanted to see you."

Rafe is checking something on his phone and might have missed the intricacies of our conversation, and he makes the off-hand comment, "We can buy anything you need once we get to Hawaii, Lexi. You don't need to pack much."

He stands and walks over to me. He's studying my expression, seeing that I'm upset even if he doesn't fully understand the emotion behind it.

I want to leave, and I can see that he's happy about this. I'm happy, too. I feel possessive of him in a new way. I want him. I want everything about him. The thought of ownership, in that moment, feels *good*. I want to be the only one who touches his thick, silky hair. His face and his smile: mine. His lips. And hands. *Mine.*

"I'll call you soon," I tell Tess.

"You better."

The elevator delivers us back to the parking lot. The driver closes the door of the limo behind us, once again sealing us into the luxurious haven. Rafe pulls me onto his lap and I let him hold me and kiss me. I let him ease my dress from my shoulders and pull it over my breasts. I let him roll the silk up my body to my waist. He lets me unfasten his jeans and hold his silken length in my hands. I straddle him and he guides his hard thickness into me, aggressively. I'm not even wet. I'm too overcome, too confused and yet not confused at all.

This visit has clarified things. I know what I want.

Him.

Even if I have no idea what it'll do to me to try something *this* outside my comfort zone.

It hurts a little, his forced, invited possession, and the tears that began when I said goodbye to Tess wet my face. I want him deeper and I ease myself up, sliding onto him, taking more of him, until he's fully inside me. Rafe takes my breasts in his hands and guides them to his mouth, sucking one flushed, sensitive nipple, then the other. He's panting lightly, groaning each time I grind my hips against him and squeeze him. I'm coming, despite the pain, and because of it. The ache is laced with shards of longing. The clenching spasms of my release are manic and wild, drawing him deeper into my body. Rafe's growl is agonized as his cock pulses inside me, filling me with liquid warmth, setting me off again into long, shimmery waves of pure pleasure.

I writhe, holding him in my arms, kissing him as yet another orgasm floods through me. My tears continue to pool, and to fall.

"It's all right," he's whispering, wiping my tears with his fingers, kissing my face. "You're all right, baby girl. I'm here now. We're together now. Everything's okay."

For now, I'll let myself believe him.

12

———

RAFE

I DIDN'T END up going into the office at all yesterday—a first—and, now, for the second day ever in my entire goddamn life, I'm completely uninterested in conquering the world of business, publishing, investments, real estate or anything else. The only thing I'm interested in conquering is Lexi's pink, perfect pussy, which is already softening under the careful marauding of my tongue.

I *really* can't fucking get enough of this girl. It's becoming a problem.

This addiction is bigger than reason. I can only hope it will begin to ease off once I sweep her away to Kauai to indulge whenever I want, without distractions.

Not that I haven't been indulging pretty much constantly since she walked into my office last Friday. And it doesn't seem to be doing anything at all to slake my desire.

In fact, it's doing the exact opposite.

The more I have of Lexi, the more I want. Every taste only makes me hungrier. Every touch only makes me more devoted. Every release only feeds my frenzy.

Like now. I eat at her like a starving man who's been given the last, ripest fruit on the very last tree: the *only* fruit. And that's the most fucked up thing about this. It almost worries me. Nothing else will *ever* taste this good. Like honey and sunshine all wrapped up into one squirming little nubile package.

I'm drifting on sensation, drugged with warm, zealous lust. My cock is hot and ferociously hard. Painful but in a lush kind of way, like I'm getting ready to burst, riding the high but holding on. I'm spilling but not yet coming.

She's awake but still drowsy. Her fingers weave themselves through my hair. She pushes weakly against my head as though to displace me.

"Rafe," she mews, scooching an inch up the bed. Retreating. "Don't."

At first I think I've misunderstood her.

Don't?

A dart of panic flickers somewhere outside the periphery of my bliss. She can't mean "don't." She probably means "more" or "faster" or "please." None of those words, true, sound anything like "don't." And she's pushing again at my head.

It's pathetic and I curse myself even as I'm doing it. I'm

about to obey her, to look up at her and see what this is about. But first I wind my hands more securely around her hips and pull her closer. I suck on her clit, circling and teasing with my tongue, hoping it'll be enough to make her forget whatever small protest she was about to make.

She moans, softly, but there's that word again. The one that makes me want to behave like some sort of psycho caveman and tie her down and *make* her give in to me. She's allowed me anything I wanted so far and the thought of her refusing me now sends a billow of dark despair through my heart.

She says my name again. Just the sound of her voice, like a wet dream on a hot night, is enough to almost fucking undo me. Again.

Hell.

It takes a ridiculous amount of effort to disengage. I look up at her. Her golden hair is all disheveled, framing her face in a wild halo. Her rose-colored lips are sultry and plump, her pale face touched by pink flashes of color just under her cheekbones. Her breasts are full and young and unbelievably beautiful.

"It's Tuesday morning." She points to her watch. Her cheap, black plastic one. It looks wrong on her peachy perfection. I put it on my mental list to buy her a gold one at my very first opportunity. "You might want to...you know. Not do that right now."

Ah. The reason we'd abandoned any pretense at birth control, after the fact.

I feel absurdly relieved. So *that's* all this is about. She's not pulling back from me or calling foul or wanting less.

She's warning me. Her time of the month is almost upon us.

Always before, with past girlfriends, any reference to the ins and outs of womanly cycles and whatnot was enough to find me extra busy at work for five solid days. Meetings and trips and so on. Disinterest spurred by the smallest amount of disgust was normal behavior. I'm a man and therefore one step removed. As it should be.

Or so I thought.

As with everything else, Lexi redefines the way I feel about this. In fact I'm more turned on than ever. The relief that cooled the poisonous effect of my initial panic feeds my fire. Milk and honey. Sweetness and sex. Life. Blood. It's all one thing. Right here in this suddenly-shy little nymphet who makes me feel more human and manly and alive than I ever have. I want to bask in her fertility. To own it.

I kiss her again, very softly. She's propped up on her elbows, watching me. "*Rafe*," she says again.

So I crawl up her body and slide my colossal cock fully into her tight little body.

"*Rafe*."

I kiss her, thrusting deeper into her. "I don't care, my sweet angel."

She likes this endearment, this reassurance. She drinks it in, like she had yesterday in the limo. For some reason, she absolutely craves these comforting murmurs.

And if there's something Lexi craves, then I'm going to fucking give it to her. As much as she wants, times ten.

"I don't think we should. It's—"

"I want you," I say again, softly, carefully, kissing her again, pushing deeper. "I won't hurt you. It'll feel good. I'll make you come, then well take a shower. I'll take care of you and give you everything you want. I'll help you pack." I punctuate each sentence with a light kiss. I can already tell she's beginning to relent. "We'll go to your doctor's appointment this morning and get your pills. I'll tie up a few loose ends in my office and we'll take the jet direct to Kauai." *I'm in hell, she feels so good.* "We can sleep on the plane. I've got a king-sized bed on my jet. You don't have to worry about anything. My house is right on the beach. We can swim at midnight. The water's beautiful and warm. I've told the housekeeper to stock the fridge with champagne and good food. I'll cook for you. I'll teach you how to surf. We can walk to the restaurant down by the resort that's nearby. I'll take care of everything. I'll take care of you."

I'm learning. I'm learning what she likes.

Her smoky green eyes are rounded and shiny. She allows me what I want, her tension easing, and her hands arc in my hair. "Rafe," she says. But this time there's no doubt in her voice. She says my name like I'm a savior and a saint, not a debauched, hedonistic addict.

I don't know what I am.

I'm not a beast, but I am completely *alive*. I'm entranced with tenderness and need. She's coming, and so am I. Like some kind of fucking Neanderthal, all I can think about is releasing my *seed* inside her. Nothing has ever felt so pure, or so *real*, as her outstanding beauty. I want it. I need it.

I love it.

Even worse, I love *her*.

I do. It hit me like a eighteen-wheeled truck from that very first moment. I can call it lust, to make it sound less heavy. But this is much more than lust.

I'm going to show her the best time of her life in Hawaii and Paris and New York and everywhere else, until she loves me back. I'm going to give her everything I have.

I love her.

I am so fucked.

SHE'S CURLED up by the window, looking out at the moonlit clouds, the darkness of the night and the reflection on the water far below.

"I can't believe we're flying over the middle of the ocean," she says in her softly-husked voice.

She was nervous about flying. She's never flown before and her vulnerabilities are more amplified tonight. She's wrapped in a quilted down comforter. I feed her bites of filet mignon I asked the chef to prepare. But she hasn't eaten much. She sips from a champagne flute.

"We're not far now," I tell her. "Do you want to sleep a little?"

"I can't sleep." She looks small and lost despite the plushness of her surroundings. I know she's never traveled before and that her excitement is laced with unease. Something about her position, with her arms hugging her bent knees like that, flicks up a haunting déjà vu. Of Max, sitting just like that, at a window in our beach shack, watching—although I hadn't known it at the time. I force the image into the dark recesses of my mind, but the protective melancholy lingers. It isn't the first time the vulnerabilities in Lexi have reminded me of my brother, who I've spent my entire life doggedly, fiercely trying to safeguard. And it makes me wonder about her. About what her insecurities stem from.

I've already admitted to myself that I love her.

And I know almost nothing about her.

I've been accused, more than once, of being disengaged from my love interests of the past. Cold workaholic. Commitment phobic. Uncaring asshole. Self-absorbed prick. I've been charged with every crime in the relationship book. And I accepted all those accusations willingly. They were true, after all. I know this about myself. Until now, I didn't feel the need to change what I assumed was just a glitch in the mechanics of my soul.

With Lexi, though, I want to learn. Everything. All of it. I want to gently, carefully dig into the painful memories in her past, whatever they might be, and fix them. With sex and diamonds and lust and clothes and love and travel and excess, I want to ease whatever burdens she carries.

For her, I want to *learn* how to love.

What bothers me is that I don't have the first goddamn clue about how to start. Love is unchartered territory for me and I'll admit the whole idea of it is fucking freaking me out. But at the same time, I'd be willing to step off the nearest cliff for this girl, with her mussed up hair and her shadowed green eyes, if she so much as asked me to.

Where to start? Something that might hint at the bigger picture, maybe. A detail that will provide the beginnings of context. Gently: "Where did you grow up, Lexi?"

I regret it instantly. It sounds strange. Overly random. But it's already out there so now I feel the need to keep going. I just want to begin. To get closer.

She stares at me—*glares*, actually—and her mouth tightens into a perfect little pout. I can see that she has no intention of answering me.

"I want some chocolate cake," she says, and the youthful petulance has returned.

All right. So she needs more time before she'll let me past even barrier number one.

I have time. I have all the time in the world.

Slices of cake were served with the meals. I go to get them, and I notice the paper bag we brought, given to Lexi after her appointment at the doctor earlier in the day. I open the bag and take out one of the birth control pills she was prescribed.

I sit down next to her, holding the pill up to her mouth. "Open. You can wash it down with the champagne."

She obeys and I places the tiny pink pill on her tongue. She takes a sip of champagne, swallowing it.

"Now you can have your cake." I feed her the chocolate cake, and she eats most of it. I want to make sure she's getting enough to eat. She seems thinner than she was even a few days ago, possibly because we've been having sex non-stop without taking regular breaks for meals. Something I'll make sure to fix once we get to Hawaii.

"How are you feeling?" I top up her champagne. "What can I get you next?"

She's watching my face, and she takes another sip of her drink. "You're so kind to me, Rafe. How did you get so kind?"

I'm not sure how to reply to this. Am I kind? In my own mind, I feel ravenously *selfish*, fixated, desperate to do anything that will get me closer to her flawlessness. To gratify myself in all the sensations of her is worth any amount of self-sacrifice. If that's what kindness is, then I can do kindness.

"I thought CEOs were supposed to be ruthless." The duvet slips off her shoulder, exposing her milky-white skin, which casts its aura over my existence, bathing me in lusty devotion.

"Oh, I'm very ruthless," I say, unable to bear this separation any longer. I lift her and place her on my lap so we can look out the window together.

She smiles, showing her white chicklet teeth. Her taunts are soft. "You're not ruthless."

"I am," I insist. "Later, I'll show you."

"Show me now." There it is. The playfulness. The girly insouciance that slays me.

"Show you now," I repeat, holding her in my arms. I could let my fingers walk a little path to where they want to go, which would tickle her and make her squirm. I could ease her knees apart and carefully, gently tug on the fine white string to slide the small cotton plug from her body. I could lift her, opening her with my fingers, fitting my cock into paradise. I could bite gently into the dewy skin of neck, until her pussy tightens around me, forcing the spooling pleasure from my cock in hot throbs.

But I don't. I get the feeling that Lexi needs a different kind of comfort right now.

She's uneasy from the flight. She hasn't eaten enough. Or slept much in the past few days.

I want to give her everything she needs…not just what *I* want her to need. Yes, this is a new look for me. For the first time in my life—aside from Max, which is a different thing altogether—I've never even *thought* of anyone else's needs. I take what I want from the people in my life and damn the consequences. So far, it's mostly worked out. But with Lexi, I want to listen. To learn. To gauge what she needs from me and provide it in spades.

Goddamn it. I care so much it hurts.

Her back rests again my chest, and I hold her more securely.

"Look," I say. I point to the white-sand coast of Kauai and the lush green craggy landscape. "There it is."

Lexi gives a delicate huff of delight. "Rafe. It's so beautiful."

Yeah, it is. And so are you. And I am so in love with you I hope like hell it doesn't end up destroying us both.

A CAR PICKS us up directly from the steps of Rafe's jet. Not a limo, but an equally-plush Range Rover type thing. I have to take exactly twelve steps on the tarmac between the plane and the car. And I know that if I ask Rafe to carry me, he'll sweep me into his burly arms without hesitating. Not that I would, but still.

It's incredibly decadent, this new luxury. Having my über-hot new lover basically at my beck and call every minute of the night and day. It's a strange feeling, especially after my former life.

I've never been so...well attended to. His alert, sapphire eyes watch me all the time. He's constantly reading me and learning me, and reacting to every new piece of myself I give him.

I already know he's obsessive, and obsessed. He's also very *protective* of me and it's this bodyguard mentality I'm almost enjoying most of all. If I felt like dwelling on the extent of it, I might be a little uneasy about how addicted I've become to the safety of him.

As we drive through the tropical jagged hills of Kauai, with their surreal coastal views, Rafe slings his burly arm around me and holds me close. "How do you like Hawaii so far?"

"It's so lush." After California and its grimy highways and arid, hazy hills, it feels like we've stepped directly onto paradise. Which I guess we kind of have.

How did my life become...*this*, and over the course of a single weekend? I've known Rafe Black for exactly five days. From couch surfing in the pink palace to a private jet to Kauai...the complete transformation of my world is giving me whiplash and I'm still adjusting. "I just never dreamed I would ever see a place like this."

"I felt the same way the first time I came to Hawaii." Rafe squeezes my hand. The one he's been holding since before we got off the plane. He's smiling at my excitement. *That* smile. The one that dazzles me every time. If anything, the more I get to know Rafe, the *more* gorgeous he gets, if such a thing is possible. Especially considering the level of gorgeousness he started at. "It was my first trip off the mainland, too, and I decided then that I needed to buy a house here so I could come here whenever I wanted to. Hawaii is where I unwind and indulge myself."

At this, our eyes meet. If he *hasn't* been indulging

himself so far and plans to start right now, then...yikes. "Yes," he murmurs into my ear, nibbling on my earlobe. "I'm dedicating this entire week to indulging myself. But most of all I'm dedicating this entire week to indulging *you.*"

Which is all cool, of course. But I can't help remembering...how we met. And why. "I'm supposed to be your new assistant," I remind him. "Do we need to be working while we're here?" I'm still wondering if he's having second thoughts about me being his new assistant, after everything that's happened. Plus, work, back in the real world, when we eventually get to it, will mean meetings and other people and...separations. Which are strangely unbearable. I cringe when I think of the only time we've socialized with other people so far. I can hardly do *that* at work. Climaxing in the middle of a board meeting might not be a great look. Then again, when the CEO is the one *giving* the orgasms... anyway, these are challenges we're going to have to figure out at some point.

"When we're ready," is all he says about that.

"When's the last time you took a week off?"

He kisses me, sucking on my bottom lip, dipping his tongue into my mouth like he can't resist the taste of me. "I have never, ever taken a week off."

"So this is a special occasion."

"Yes."

"What *is* the occasion?" Just to hear him say it.

"*You*, my delectable Lexi," he says against my mouth, his fingers tugging gently on my nipple through the thin fabric of yet another new top. "The sweetest little goddamn occasion in the entire fucking universe."

He kisses me deeply then, pushing his tongue into me like he does when he's inside me, as he pulls me onto his lap. His hard length wedges itself against me, fitting intimately in a way that never fails to drive me wild. I'm wearing a short, frilly white skirt that rides up easily under his wandering hands.

But I'm also distracted. "*Rafe*, is this your *house*?" It's big and sort of glowing in the soft Hawaiian sunlight, but also quaint and inviting, built in the plantation style and painted a very pale shade of yellow with white trim. Its front yard is a wide, golden sugar-sand beach dotted with palm trees. I honestly don't think I could have dreamed up a house that's as perfect as this house. Not to mention a location that's basically to die for. I'm speechless, it's so beautiful.

The car pulls to a stop at the front door.

"*Fuck*," he says under his breath, and I think he might be referring to his monster erection. "Yeah, this is it."

"We're here," I say helpfully.

He looks at me like he's considering locking the doors, holding me down behind the tinted windows and having his way with me, waiting chauffeur and beckoning waves be damned.

"Down boy," I tease him, because just *look* at this place. I don't actually think I've ever been as excited as I am right now.

"I'll down boy you, darlin', as soon as I get half a chance."

This isn't the first time I've detected the slightest note of a southern-type drawl in the inflections of Rafe's speech. Texas, maybe. It makes me wonder about his past. His childhood. Aside from the obvious details of his success and his wealth, it's true that I know almost nothing else about him. He has a brother. He owns a number of companies. He went to Stanford.

Neither of us likes talking about our pasts, that's obvious. I know *I* don't, and he seems just as cagey about his. I'm fine with that, but given the intensity of our relationship, eventually—if there is an "eventually"—we might have to begin to share more about who we are. The thought makes me uneasy, so I push it aside. This place is too stunning to worry about things like that today.

I shimmy off of his lap, rearranging my clothing.

"You just wait," he's muttering. "I'm going to lock you away for the entire week and do whatever I want to you, whenever I want. With no distractions and no interruptions."

"Sure you can, Rafey," I tease him, laughing at the aroused, disheveled state of him. The door is being opened by the oblivious driver, and I take my opportunity to step out onto the driveway.

Rafe climbs out of the car and stands next to me. His black hair and white teeth and the obvious detail that he's super-rich make him glow like a sparkling, preppy pirate king. Everything about him screams alpha. He holds his jacket in front of him to attempt to shield the not-so-small detail of his gargantuan hard-on. But then when we get closer to the door—and I'm a little starstruck by every detail of this place—he says, "Fuck it," and drops his jacket. Then he scoops me into his arms before carrying me over the threshold.

"Rafe," I protest. It's not like we're newlyweds or anything. But he ignores my protests. To his chauffeur and the two women who must be his housekeepers, ready to bow to His Majesty's every demand, he says, "Take our things to the master bedroom and have a bottle of champagne chilling on the patio. Then everyone can take the rest of the week off, fully paid, of course. If we need more provisions, I'll let you know. Until then, Lexi and I can handle things from here."

"Certainly, Mr. Black," one of them says. They follow his orders immediately, disappearing.

I can't help but notice he sounded sort of gruff. He's grumpy, maybe, since his hard-on isn't being attended to.

He's still carrying me.

"No 'please'? Do you always speak to people like that?"

"I only say please to you."

"That's rude," I tell him.

"You don't know the half of how *rude* I am, honey." He spins the word to sound positively filthy, and his lips curve in a smile that promises as much as I can handle. "But you'll soon find out."

"I want you to teach me to surf."

"Yes, we'll get to all that—"

"Now."

He stares down at me. Clearly, he had other activities on his mind. I'm not entirely sure why, but I want to test him. I know he's controlling. I know he's somewhat addicted (okay, more than "somewhat") to our physical connection. What I'm wondering is: how far will he go?

Can I...*control* him? I guess I'm wondering how uneven this balance of power is. If he'll allow me to call some of our shots. Because if there's any chance of making this "thing" between us actually work for...the foreseeable future, then he's going to have to. I'm a person who's basically been entirely independent since I was seven years old. And right now I feel surly, strung out from the travel and the fact that *I'm in freaking Hawaii!*, and a million miles from the subservience he seems to always demand.

He kisses me. "I was going to suggest I give you a tour of the master bedroom and its California king."

"We'll get to all that," I say, repeating his words. "But

first I want to freshen up, put on my bikini and go for a swim."

I'm not going to say I'm surprised by what he does next, but some little fissure in my heart opens when he gently sets me down. "Take as long as you need, Miss Blondeau. The master bedroom is at the top of the stairs to the right. Your bags will already be up there. I'll be waiting for you on the patio, glass of champagne and some brunch at the ready."

"Thank you, Mr. Black."

He smiles and his eyes do that smoldering thing again. Then he watches me walk up the stairs (I know, because I glance back at him and he's gorgeous, standing there all unruly and turned on), then I go and find his bedroom. I'm glad to have a few minutes to myself to just gather my thoughts and adjust to all this.

This place.

It's unreal.

The house has been renovated to make the most of the old-school charm while also ramping up every modern, luxurious detail. The beams that run the length of the vaulted ceilings have been painted white, giving the space a clean, airy feel. There's a sitting area with plush couches set into a spacious little alcove that makes the most of the view. French doors lead out to a balcony that looks over the beach and out to sea. It must be a private beach, because there's not a single person on it. Far into the distance, I can see tiny red umbrellas set out in front of what looks like a resort. It's the only other sign of civilization and, at a guess, is probably a couple of miles away.

His bed, as promised, is huge and covered in mountains of white pillows and duvets clearly made from the highest thread-count Egyptian cotton money can buy. I'm tired and the whole ensemble looks wildly inviting, but I can hear the lapping of the waves. It's a beautiful day in Kauai and I'm way too excited to sleep.

The *extravagance*. It's hard to get used to so *much* of it. I walk into the master bathroom, which is the size of Tess's entire apartment. The bathroom has an enormous jacuzzi bath and a state-of-the-art shower. The furnishings and all the decorative touches are the most romantic and at the same time the most expensive I have ever seen.

Holy hell.

I change into one of my new bikinis, which is minuscule and a leopard print, then put on a little sundress Rafe (also) bought me. It's lacy white cotton and sort of sheer. It only comes to the very top of my thighs, but at least it's a layer. I have the feeling if I go down there with only my bikini on, I won't get my surfing lesson until much later.

I go down the curving staircase and give myself a short tour. There's a media room with a wall-mounted state-of-the-art-looking TV and huge cream-colored squashy couches, a living room with more couches and chairs and modern, cool furniture. Folding doors have been fully opened onto the patio, which has palm trees and an infinity pool, a raised hot tub and several seating areas looking out over the view of the beach and the water.

This house is quite literally perfect.

Like everything else in his world.

Rafe's not on the patio so I keep wandering and find him in the kitchen. It's as over-the-top as I've now come to expect.

He's cooking.

"I hope you like omelets."

I smile. I was so not expecting this. He looks hot and beautiful and...much more than that. He's wearing only a pair of blue board shorts and his hair is wet from a swim in the pool. I love that he seems so out of place cooking, like he's a little unsure of himself. He checks the omelet to make sure it's not burning and when he takes the toast out of the toaster, he drops it onto a plate before shaking his hand a little and sucking on his finger. "Ouch."

I laugh. His chest hair and his muscles and the way his damp shorts are hanging low on his hips, and everything else about him is just so...outrageously *male*. "I didn't know you could cook."

"Sure I can. I make a mean omelet," he says defensively, as though insulted by my comment, which makes me laugh again.

"I'm starving."

"You haven't been eating enough, which is something

we will remedy completely this week. Champagne?" I notice he's already poured two glasses. One of them is only half full. He hands me the other one.

I sit on a tall stool so I can watch him. "For breakfast? I don't want to fall off my surfboard."

"You can have one glass. We're on vacation. Which I've never been on before. We're going to make the most of it."

He's never taken a vacation. Until me. It's a heady thought, that *I* have this kind of power over him, to make him drop his billionaire lifestyle and his company/magazine/investment portfolio to fly me to Hawaii just so he give me surf lessons and cook me omelets. And keep me all to himself.

"Thank you for bringing me here, Rafe. I love it."

He clinks his glass against mine. "Thank you for coming with me. I love having you here with me. This house is my sanctuary."

"I can see why."

Something passes between us as we sip the bubbling champagne. A connective, visceral tenderness. The champagne tastes good. Just a few sips of it gives me a light buzz. Probably because this is breakfast and all I had for dinner was a few bites of filet mignon and some chocolate cake. I sip again.

Rafe serves up the buttery toast and cheese omelets and glasses of freshly-squeezed orange juice and we take everything out to the patio where we sit and eat. It's delicious, simple food and it's nice to have something familiar and normal amid all the OTT grandeur.

"See that break out there?" Rafe points out to the water, where a curling wave begins close to a small island, then tubes itself along the ocean for a good hundred feet or more. "It's the perfect wave to learn on because it's not too big and if you fall off it's just soft sand underneath. That's part of the reason I bought this house. It's always there, just like that. In the winter months, the surf is a lot bigger."

"When did you learn to surf?"

"When I was about thirteen. I was obsessed with it when I was younger. Then other things got in the way and I didn't have time. Once business picked up, I decided to buy myself a surf spot. When I saw this place, I knew it was perfect."

When business picked up. I wonder if he means after he became a billionaire, or maybe it was when he was still only a multi-millionaire. "I can understand why people get practically religious about it," I say. "Riding that huge, powerful surge of clear blue water like you own it, even for a couple of seconds, it must be such a rush."

He's smiling, like he finds my philosophical outburst wildly fascinating. "It *is* a rush. The second-best feeling in the world. Some people even say it's the best feeling in the world, but then they obviously haven't met Lexi Blondeau."

He's teasing me again, and I have a flashback to a

particularly debauched thing he did *with his tongue* and feel myself blush. But I smile back at him. I can't help it. "Can we go surfing now?"

"Finish your breakfast. You need energy to surf." He's bossy but relaxed about it. Both of us are fully aware that he's giving me time to adjust to him. I know what *he'd* rather be doing right now and there's a thrill to the way he's watching me, like a tiger who plays with its food before eating it.

A very *evolved* tiger.

One that knows if he plays *too* hard, his food might just...run away. Or something. I don't mind being Rafe Black's captive. But there are limits to what I can handle. To his credit, he seems to understand this. He's giving me time.

We finish eating and we clear the table and take the dishes into the kitchen. "I like getting all domestic with you," he says, leaning to kiss my neck. "This is a first for me, by the way."

"You don't bring...other women here?"

God, why did I just ask him that? First of all, I don't want to know. Second, he probably wouldn't tell me anyway. But then he says, "No. I've never brought anyone here besides Max."

He's eyeing me.

Smirking. "You have no idea how happy it makes me that you're jealous at the thought of me bringing 'other women' here or anywhere else. Your jealousy is adorable. It makes me want to go all caveman on you."

He seems to be waiting for a response. "Caveman?" is the best I can come up with.

"Yes." He weaves a finger lightly around an end strand of my hair. "I'm very tempted indeed to sling you over my shoulder, carry you up to my bedroom and fuck you senseless."

Oh. I'm a little shocked, but I get over it. I'm getting used to him. "I'm not jealous," I lie.

"You are." Smugly.

I've always been told I'm easy to read and with someone as perceptive as Rafe, I might as well have a tattoo across my forehead saying *okay, yes, I might have been just the tiniest bit jealous at the thought. Actually, more than a tiny bit. I hate the thought of you with "other women."* It's irritating that I can't ever mask my feelings. "It's none of my business what you do—or did—with other women. Mr. Black." My comment sounds barely petulant, which amuses him.

"I'm glad you clarified the past tense, Miss Blondeau. Because I'm distractingly—and, if you really want to know, alarmingly—besotted with only one woman and she's the one I'm about to give surf lessons to...unless you want to take me up on my other offer?" His sincere hopefulness at the question sort of slays me a little.

"I'll start with the surf lesson."

He laughs, but his eyes still have that tiger thing going on, which is both freaking me out and turning me on like crazy. It's not fair that he's so ridiculously hot *and* that he also has all these layers to his personality that, as each one is revealed to me, only makes me...*like?...want?...crave?* him more. I don't even know the right word for what I feel for Rafe.

He takes my hand and leads me out onto the patio and down a sandy path where there's a large, locked shed. Inside, there are surfboards, jet skis, kayaks, paddle boards, an all-terrain vehicle and a small boat. He chooses two boards. "Long boards are better on smaller waves and they're easier to learn on," he says. "You do know how to swim, right? Or should I put a life jacket on you?"

"I know how to swim."

"Good. I need you safe. I have big plans for you later."

"I have some plans for you, too," I tell him. This new boldness is something I'm still adjusting to. I bite my lip. His eyes flash again and I wonder what it'll take to push him past his breaking point. I almost want to try to do it. To tempt him in a way that makes him break down...and sling me over his shoulder, carry me up to his bedroom and fuck me senseless.

I'm pretty sure I could tempt that breaking point very easily.

But then he starts walking down to the water, carrying both boards, as though he's unaffected...except he can't really hide the gigantic ridge in his shorts. I catch up to him and when I laugh he gives me a tortured look.

God, I love being with him. He's funny and he's fun.

And I fall just a little deeper. Disconcertingly, I know this is only the tip of the iceberg of how hard I could fall for this guy. *You mean how hard you already* are *falling for this guy,* my subconscious points out, *who can and probably will break your heart about ten different ways.*

Anyway, I'm here, learning to surf, and it's just about the best thing that's ever happened to me so I'm not going to second-guess everything. At least not right now.

Rafe lays both surfboards on the sand. He spends a while teaching me the right stance and how to stand up and keep my balance.

He's patient. And he's a good teacher. He adjusts my arms and shows me where to place my feet. "I'll be right there with you the whole time. Now," he says, once he's satisfied I've got the details right. "Take this off." He pulls my dress up over my head.

His hard-on—which has been absurdly obvious the entire time—gets even more gargantuan. Good thing his shorts are sturdy-looking, otherwise he'd be busting right out of them. My bikini is basically a couple of shreds of strategically-placed fabric and it's been almost twelve hours since either of us have...gotten off, I guess you could say. A record for us.

We're both ignoring the beast in his shorts. He's being

so good. So easy-going. He's almost behaving like a normal person, even though the smoky burn in his eyes hints at the volatility going on behind that mostly-impassive expression.

I might be a little bit of a sadist but at least I'm not the only one. Even as it occurs to me that it might be a little bit cruel (in a good way), I want to see how much he can handle. It's not like *he's* not testing *me* at every turn. We're even, I figure. I brush my barely-concealed nipples against his chest as I stand on my tippy-toes to place a light kiss on his mouth. Have I mentioned how much I *love* his mouth? It's perfectly-shaped and—even if I didn't have intimate knowledge of just how debauched it actually is—you can just tell it would be.

"After we surf," I say, "maybe we could take a little nap. Since we didn't sleep much on the plane."

Oh...*holy shit*. His eyes positively *flare* with lust.

But then he catches himself. He shrugs and one of his eyebrows barely lifts as he gives me a sardonic glare. "Maybe."

I smile at him. He's meeting my challenge head on.

In fact, if I don't focus here, he's going to beat me at my own game. Of resisting. I want to take his big cock out of his shorts now. To play with him and suck on him until he's totally overcome.

But then he'd win.

So I kiss his mouth once more before stepping away to get my board.

He stands there for a few seconds, panting lightly. He bends forward, and rests his hands on his knees. "You're going to kill me, you know that, right?"

"I'll make it up to you. Come on." I smile at him. "I'm ready."

He murmurs something like, *oh, you'll be ready all right,* but he grabs his board and we wade into the calm water. It feels like bath water. It's the exact same temperature as the air.

This place really is paradise.

Especially with my new surf instructor Billionaire McHottie completing the panorama. He shows me how to paddle out toward the wave.

"You go first," I tell him.

Rafe explains to me about the timing and the placement I'm looking for and then he paddles out and, just at the right moment, jumps onto his board and surfs the wave.

Wow.

He's beyond glorious.

Then, after he's showed me the technique, he dives off his board and swims over to me, flicking his hair out of his eyes when he resurfaces in that way hot guys do. He looks younger like this, and, even though my subconscious is shouting her mantra again, *tread carefully, girl, this guy is waaay too good to be true*, I can't help myself: I kiss him, this beautiful bastard who has somehow become the most important thing in my life in only five short days.

"Your turn," he says.

I try a few times and don't quite time it right but then Rafe paddles with me and, somehow *I do it!* I stand up just like he showed me and find my balance and...holy hell, *I'm surfing!* And he's right, it's just about the best feeling I've ever had.

No, he's also right: the second best feeling.

I ride the wave for a total of approximately three seconds before I fall off. When I swim back to him, he's smiling. "You did it, baby. That was so good."

I'm ridiculously excited. "I did, didn't I, Rafe? I really did it!"

"You're a natural, sweetheart."

Rafe kisses me and our tongues dance silkily. We're so *happy*. It might just be the most magical moment of my life. All because of him.

"Do it again," he says.

We spend the next few hours surfing and I manage to catch a few good rides. Rafe shows off some of his moves. He tells me he got sponsorship for his surfing when he was sixteen and considered making a career out of it. But he wanted to make more money than surfing would provide, he said. He wanted an empire. So, after college, he moved to L.A. and started building one.

He doesn't tell me where he moved from and I don't ask. Little by little, we're starting to let each other in, and I get that uneasy feeling I always do when I share details of myself. It's a door I prefer to keep closed.

We start getting hungry again and decide to go and have a late lunch.

We paddle in to shore and Rafe puts our boards away. We make some lunch and sit out and watch the waves breaking as Rafe opens another bottle of champagne.

After we eat, he says, "Are you ready for that nap now?"

Rafe's eyes meet mine and they're dark.

He takes my glass of champagne, which is almost empty. "I want you to go upstairs and wait for me in my bed. Make sure there's nothing on you, or in you, that might present a barrier to me. Take all the time you need."

It's been nice to spend time with him that's not *only* about our crazy physical attraction. To let the anticipation build and slowly burn. But now that we have, my lust for him has taken on a new edge. A deeper edge.

I stand up, still wearing only my bikini. I kiss him lightly and he slips his strong hand around the nape of my neck and holds me there, kissing me deeply, passionately.

"See you soon," I say, and I can tell he's getting close to some kind of threshold. He seems barely able to control himself. "Give me five minutes."

I smile at him as I retreat and make my way upstairs.

Rafe had bought me several new travel bags—wildly

expensive ones, of course—and the smaller of the two had been placed in the bathroom by his staff.

I take a quick shower to wash the salt off. I wrap a towel around me and open the door leading into his bedroom. Rafe's standing out on the balcony, looking at the view. I go to him.

He looks down at me, and pulls me against the hard planes of his body. "I'm going to ravage you, sweet Lexi, until you can barely remember your own name. Are you ready for me?" He unwraps my towel and tosses it over a chair. Then he kneels down in front of me, holding me in place with his hands. Good thing this is a private beach. He kisses the soft cove between my legs, once, and again. The cocktail of lust, champagne, sleep deprivation, exercise and jet lag compounds to give reality a sumptuous, luminous tint. I felt lucky and playful and supremely alive.

I squirm from his hold. "*No*, Rafe," I remind him softly.

He grabs for me, but I dart in through the door, standing behind one of the couches, ready to bolt.

"Lexi," he says sternly, standing in the doorway. He's in no mood for games.

He walks toward me, skirting the couch to get closer. But I move, too, keeping just out of reach and a laugh escapes me. He takes off his shorts.

Sweet Jesus.

He's so turned on, his cock touches his stomach. It's

all...engorged and slick with moisture. "Come here. Or I'll have to take you over my knee."

I want to tease him.

I touch myself, fingering my nipples. "Is *this* what you want, Rafey?"

He goes very still. He takes a step closer.

I let my hands slide slowly down my stomach and across my hips as he watches me. I want to drive him crazy. I lick one of my fingers, touching it to my softness. "Or *this*?" I gasp a little as the warmth rises under the touch of my own fingers. "You should feel how hot and wet I am."

He exhales in a barely-spoken breath.

His eyes are darker than I've ever seen them. He looks mean and dangerously aroused.

But still, I want to push him. To ignite him. To play with my own power. To somehow push him further than he's ever been pushed. "Because you know this is all yours, don't you, Rafe?" I say softly. "Yours." I touch my sensitive nipples. "Yours." I touch my fingers *there*, "And this. All soft and ready for you. Yours."

I walk over to the bed, sliding onto my hands and knees. He's already there, and his thick cock thrusts into me from behind as his hands push my body into the position he demands. My shoulders are held down so my face is pressed against the covers. He pulls my hips higher and forces my knees further apart. Rafe's hands hold me down in a vice-grip that feels on the verge of bruising me as he drives into me, thick and deep. I cry out at the unexpected ferocity of him. If I was attempting to push him past some unknowable boundary, I've succeeded. He's never been *this* forceful with me before. His massive, rigid cock pushes roughly into me, again and again, reaching deeper with each lunge. When I reach back to touch some part of him in an unspoken plea to slow down, to be more gentle, he grabs both my hands, clinching my wrists behind my back in one of his fists. The combined force of his depth, his thickness, his grip and the driving pace is too much. I'm wet but still too-tight and sensitive, and the sliding friction is edged with pain. I'd forgotten how unbelievably strong he is.

"*Rafe*," I gasp.

It takes him a few seconds to slow, almost like he's having trouble pulling himself out of a delirium of total, blind dominance. But then his movements slow. He curls his body over mine, resting his head against my back. He kisses my shoulder. "I'm sorry," he murmurs.

"Don't hurt me," I whisper.

"I won't." I can hear the remorse in his voice but also the thrumming voltage of his need. He'll go easier on me, but he won't be denied. I almost wonder what would happen if I asked him to stop, now. Would he? I get the feeling he wouldn't. That he *couldn't*. I don't *want* him to stop but this edge of doubt makes my heart beat faster.

"You're just so fucking gorgeous," he says, kissing and

biting my skin. "I want you so much, baby. I want to eat you and drink you and live inside you. I'm going mad, sweet girl. I can't handle this. I can't handle *you*. Do you want me, Lexi? Do you want me?"

I do want him. Of course I do. So much. Too much.

He doesn't wait for my answer, and I don't expect him to. He slides deeper, pressing his hips against me in a tender but very persuasive thrust. As he does, he groans loudly. Anguished: that's how he sounds. Like he's lost himself. This time, his thickness rubs a charged place inside me. He does it again, thrusting, seeking in the last inch of his drive an insanely intimate trigger. And finding it. A sweet, warm ache begins to build deep inside me.

"Lexi?" he whispers, thrusting again. His words are slurred with lust. "Okay, baby?"

"Yes," I moan, not caring anymore about gentleness or boundaries. He's breaking me open, flooding my body and soul with hard beauty. I don't care if he can't stop himself. *I* can't either. If he pulled himself away now I would die. The physicality of our need has taken a turn. *"Yes, Rafe. Please."*

He pulls out a little, but not all the way, immediately pushing back in, stoking the fire. With each plunge, he retreats a fraction less, until the cyclical glide isn't a with-drawal at all, but one dynamic, rolling thrust that stays with me, never leaving the stroking contact of that deep, perfect sweetspot. The pleasure grows, inflaming my body, and I'm pushing my hips back against him as he plays this beautiful rhythm. My arms slide to the bed, giving me leverage to push back against him. His fingers find across my slippery center of sensation, and his other thumb is wet and sliding just barely into the secret puckered cove of my ass, not entering me there but rubbing gently.

The pleasure compounds, riding a silky wave, coasting then breaking with a force that sends a flurry of stars through my brain and my body that I can feel in zapping surges all the way to my fingertips and toes. I'm riding some ultimate high. My inner muscles draw lusciously around his massive, pulsing cock until he groans and lays his body heavily over mine, gripping me as his climax racks through him.

After he calms, he rolls us to our sides so his arms and legs are fully wrapped around me, spooning me, still inside me.

There are tears in my eyes and I'm not sure why. My chest feels heavy with a strange new longing. I don't even understand my own emotions. They're too raw and too new. We lie like that for a while, catching our breath and recovering from the crazy intensity of our lovemaking.

"What's my name again?"

"Told you," he murmurs against my hair, stroking with careful, supplicating tenderness. As though to make amends. "Gorgeous Lexi."

I don't answer him. I've already forgiven him, if that's

what's even required here. I'm not sure and I don't care. I already knew I was in for a wild ride with him, physically, emotionally, psychologically, existentially. All of it. *Let's not forget the icing on the cake*, I thought. *Financially.*

I force that thought out of my head. I don't want anything about this to be about money. I just want to be as close to him as possible.

We sleep for a while, spent and still connected. I wake when I feel Rafe slide from my body. "Let's take a bath," he says, walking into the bathroom.

He calls me in when it's ready, and he's already in it, leaning back, up to his neck in bubbles, his black hair flicked with frothy suds. Something about this big, CEO sex god taking a bubble bath strikes me as not only funny but...cute.

"Come here," he says.

I climb in, getting ready to lean back toward the opposite end.

"Over here," he insists. "Come lean against me."

So I lie against Rafe's chest and he begins to soap me, rubbing a soft sea sponge against my skin. Not lustily, for once, but gently, just gliding it across my breasts and my body.

The windows are open and I can hear the sound of the waves.

"Where were you born?" he asks quietly.

So we're back to twenty questions. He's caught me at a

better moment this time. If I want to find out more about him, I guess it's only reasonable that I start to open up to him, too. Within reason. "You first."

He seems encouraged by this although there's a reserve in him that I recognize, only because I know all about reserve. Maybe his story isn't an easy one either. "Texas."

"You grew up in Texas? I wouldn't have picked you for Texas." Although, I have heard it: hints of that cowboy twang that surface every now and then. Mainly when he's lust-drunk. When his guard is completely down.

"We lived in Houston until I was ten. Then we moved to Florida and stayed there until I was seventeen." The comment is laced with all kinds of craziness: anger, regret, matter-of-fact grit. I can sense that Rafe's road has not been smooth. Something I can definitely relate to. I'm curious but I don't want to push him. I wait for him to continue but he says, "Your turn."

"A small town in eastern Oregon," I say quietly. "I was born in my mother's house. I arrived so quickly she didn't have time to drive to the hospital." I'm a little amazed with myself. I've never told that detail to anyone. Not that it's all that earth-shattering, but still. And then I hear myself say, "She was alone."

I wait for the obvious question and it's not long before he asks it. "Where was your father?"

"He was already gone by then. He left a few months

before I was born. I never met him. He never came back. I never even saw a picture of him. She burned them all."

Rafe's quiet for a few seconds, just gliding the sponge over my shoulder and down my arm. "I'm sorry."

I suddenly don't want to talk about any of this anymore. I don't want my dismal past infecting this perfect moment. My past is behind me, right where it belongs. "What's your favorite color?" I ask him, changing the subject.

"Black."

"Black's not a color."

"I still like it."

"What's your second favorite color?"

"Blue. What's yours?"

"Red. And pink."

"Actually," he says. "Pink is my favorite color, too." He touches a wet finger to my lips. "This pink." His other hand slides lower, over my breast, where he swirls a finger around my soapy nipple. "And this pink." His touch wanders lower, down my stomach, and lower, not with possessive intention but with more of a tender adoration. "And this pink."

I let him touch me possessively, almost off-handedly. I don't know if I should feel concerned or happy about the fact that I'm his and we've both just accepted that. "What kind of music do you like?"

"The Rolling Stones. And Mozart. My taste in music is sort of old school."

I look up at him and he softly, softly kisses my lips.

"I'll tell you what," he says. "I'm going to tell you about myself. I'm going to tell you things I've never told anyone. I want you to know who I am."

"Only if you want to, Rafe," I whisper.

"I do. And you're going to tell me things, too. About you. I want to know you. I want to know what makes you laugh and what haunts you. I get that things haven't always been easy for you, Lexi. I want to share your heartbreak and ease every hardship you've ever had. I want you to let me do that."

Is this guy even real? My own personal knight in shining armor.

We both have secrets, that's obvious. The thought of sharing with him, of opening myself up to him emotionally as well as physically feels less daunting than it did only days ago. Knowing that he has his own scars makes me feel like we're on equal footing. And it makes this relationship feel like it's about more than just sex.

But still, I'm too used to being alone, and entirely self-sufficient. And to keeping my secrets hidden.

This is a different side of Rafe. His sincerity is bringing out his softer, more romantic tendencies. After the force of his lovemaking, the words sound doubly sweet. First he broke me open with his lust and now he's planting little love seeds in the fresh dirt.

"So?" he says. "Your favorite music? Your go-to movies? Books that are dog-eared on your bedside table?" He seems to understand that keeping things light will get better results.

"I have very eclectic tastes in music," I tell him, crossing some sort of divide. A warm, trickling emotion is filling me. In my throat and in the low pit of my stomach. *I love him. I absolutely love him. And I barely know him.* "I like the blues. I read a lot, of everything. The goods and the greats, but also the best-sellers, which one of my teachers called the 'cornerstones of the modern American zeitgeist', which I liked the sound of."

"I sometimes forget that you're a scholar as well as a supermodel sex kitten," he says, kissing me again. "You can play me some of your playlists."

"I don't have any."

"What? Why not?"

"My phone is so outdated it can only handle the basics. I've been meaning to upgrade so I can get more apps." I don't go into detail about how ridiculously limited my budget in college was. My old phone has definitely seen better days and possibly better decades.

"I'll get you a new one."

"No, Rafe. That's not what I meant. You don't need to keep buying me things."

"What's wrong with me buying you things?"

"It makes me feel like we're on uneven ground."

"Well, you need to get over that," he says, squeezing my nipple intimately, possessively. "If there's any uneven ground here, it's that you're standing on Mt. Everest and I'm floundering around in the Mariana Trench."

I gasp a small laugh as his fingers play.

"It's the deepest point in the ocean," he informs me.

"I think I've heard of it."

"Did you know that if Mt. Everest was put into the trench, its peak would still be a mile underwater?"

"I did not know that, no. And I don't really think your analogy is accurate."

Rafe pulls me up so I'm on top of him, facing him. He adjusts us, fitting his huge cock so it's pressing strongly against me. "All this talk about underwater trenches is getting me hot," he says.

"You're always hot."

"That's because you *make* me hot, baby. So hot I can't fucking breathe."

"You're going to splash all the water out." I moan as he enters me. Carefully, I sit up onto him, taking him deeper. And deeper. My breasts are wet and flecked with bubbles. My dripping hair brushes against his chest.

"Lexi?"

"Yeah?"

"I love you."

I stare at him for a few seconds, then I lean onto him and kiss him as he grips me with his hands and thrusts hard. I'm already coming and crying a little and kissing him like I'm trying to take his words back.

I don't know if I can handle this, even if I love him, too. I do, already, and I don't know if I *want* to love him. It's too quick.

Can this last?

Can it stay this good?

If I let him into my heart, it'll kill me. When he leaves, it'll shatter me into a million tiny, unfixable pieces. And I don't *want* to break into a million tiny, unfixable pieces.

Can I trust him with my heart?

Or should I walk away before it becomes impossible?

14

OVER THE NEXT WEEK, Rafe and I retreat into our intimate bubble. We cook together. We make love. We surf. We swim. We make love again. We live in our bathing suits, or nothing at all. Our skin gets tan and our hair is sandy.

He doesn't push me to talk about things I don't want to talk about. I can sense that he's frustrated by this, but there are some lines I just don't want to cross, especially not here and now, and he backs off. We talk about the weather, my surfing technique, movies we've watched. He doesn't tell me he loves me again and I'm relieved by this.

I don't know how to feel, so I just live entirely in the moment. These moments are the best I've ever had, so it's easy enough to do.

After taking me so roughly on that first day, he's gentler now, mostly, but there's an edge to him. I'm immersed in the beautiful, strengthening bond between us, but I notice it. It ghosts at the fringes. Off-hand remarks that are easily overlooked between the Bollinger and the warm ocean water and the full-body orgasms.

You're mine.

You're moving in with me as soon as we get back to L.A.

I'm never letting you out of my sight.

I go with it, but I wonder how it'll all play out once we're back in real life. It's easy enough to give myself to him entirely in Hawaii, but things will have to change once we're back at work, with business meetings and schedules to keep and inevitable separations.

I know his obsession borders on the extreme. But I can't quite bring myself to worry about this. I can't fault him for his dedication to me, can I? Besides, I *like* that he's attentive and possessive. I'm sort of basking in his adoration, because it's so new to me. He's loving and sweet and... well, hot as fuck. If anything, I encourage him, by teasing him and inviting him at every opportunity I get.

It's not a one-way thing. We're addicted to each other.

It's just after breakfast on our seventh day in Hawaii. "We're going to go out on the boat today," he says.

"You have a boat?" He might be talking about the one I'd seen in the shed. "That sounds fun."

"It's over at the marina. We'll stay on it tonight."

He drives us to the marina and parks the Range Rover

before leading me along the narrow winding docks to one of the bigger spaces. "This is it."

My jaw actually drops. "Rafe. This isn't a boat. This is a *yacht*. A very *huge* yacht."

"Yeah," he says, blasé, like why *wouldn't* we be spending time on what's basically a massive multi-million dollar toy that he occasionally uses when he just happens to be in the mood? "Come on."

Holy shit, is what I'm thinking, as he leads me aboard. It's a *super*-yacht, the kind with its own crew and kitchen and pool. There's a hot tub on the deck next to the built-in, cushioned seating area. There's a lounge inside with big windows, couches and a dark-wood bar area.

"The bedrooms are down below," he says. "There are five of them.

Five?

"I rent this boat out when I'm not using it. It's an investment, Lexi. You can close your mouth now."

Oh. Oops. Am I that obvious, that this is all just a little... overwhelming?

"Right after I do this." He gently pats my cheek. Then he holds my jaw, easing it almost closed. He takes my mouth in a searing kiss, his tongue lusty and demanding. Then he pulls back, gazing at me in a half-stern, half-cocky challenge to resist him.

I can't. I suddenly need him with a ferocity I don't understand. The kiss. That *taste* of him and his scent...it reminds me of that very first time I saw him. Of our overblown reaction to each other. Of how good and how desired and how safe he makes me feel. "Can you show them to me?"

"Show what to you?"

"I want to see your bedroom."

He cocks his head and stares at me sharply as my words sink in, then he pulls me by the hand through the lounge and down a staircase into a large bedroom with a king-sized bed and two round windows that are half-submerged. He closes the door and locks it. He lifts me, pressing me against the door, pulling up my mini-dress and ripping off my panties as he plunges his big, thick length all the way inside me. *Oh god, it's too big.* Too hard. He's forcing his way inside and it's too much. This couldn't even be called lovemaking. He's *fucking* me and it's hard and rough and each thrust forces the excruciating plea-sure-pain higher. And higher. I cry out as the ecstasy crashes through me and my inner muscles grip him over and over in tight, clenching pulls until he's growling against my neck, *Lexi, oh Lexi, oh, God, I can't take this*, and his cock is jerking inside me.

We stay there, just like that, panting for a few minutes, still almost fully clothed. Then he smooths a strand of damp hair back from my face. He seems almost pissed off. He pulls out of me and the wetness spills as he sets me down onto my feet. *Yikes.* He uses my ripped panties to clean some of his cum that's wetting my thighs. Then he stuffs them into his pocket.

He pulls my dress down to cover me. Then he steps away from me and buttons up his shorts. "*Fuck*, Lexi."

I'm not sure what he's mad about. Maybe the fact that we basically can't keep our hands—or anything else—off each other? It's crazy and uncontrollable and totally inappropriate. Or at least it will be when we're in any situation that doesn't involve private beach houses and/or yachts.

"Do you *know* what you *do* to me?" he says gruffly. "I don't *want* to be rough with you! You drive me insane! I'm losing my fucking mind!" He grabs a fistful of his hair.

He's sort of looming over me, aggressively. "Rafe. I...I *wanted* you to do all that."

"*No.* I was too fucking rough! I *hurt* you, I could *hear* that."

"You didn't hurt me, Rafe. It felt...*good*. More than good."

Dramatically, he drops to his knees in front of me and hugs his arms around my legs, resting his head against me. "I'm completely losing my grip, baby. I can't seem to control myself with you. I want you so much. I need to... *God damn it all to hell!* I need to calm the fuck down."

Okay, maybe just a little.

I weave my fingers through his hair. He seems so anguished and I understand it. It's more intensity than either of us knows what to do with.

He stands and looks down at me, holding my face in his hands, gently this time. His eyes are full of awe. "I know you don't want me to say it, sweet girl, but I have to. I need to let it out because it's too much to keep in. I *love* you and it's the most extreme thing that's ever happened to me. I don't know how to deal with the fucking *extent* of it. I'm still trying to figure that out. But I'll try harder. Please forgive me."

"Rafe." *Oh my god.* He loves me. And he wants me to *forgive* him for that? It's so sudden and confusing and life-changing. "There's nothing to forgive."

He kisses me again. The kiss is tender and passionate and full of devotion. "Are you sure you're all right?"

"Yes." I hesitate, but then it sort of tumbles out. I want to give this to him, even though it hurts my heart to say it, because letting the words out only makes it feel more real. "I love you."

As long as I live, I will never forget the look on his face. The billionaire alpha literally brought to his knees. This complicated, volatile, beautiful man, speechless with awe.

He carefully lifts me into his arms. My chest feels tight and sort of heavy with love for him. I'm crying. I love him so much it literally hurts. "I'll be better at controlling myself, I promise," he says. "I'm going to take such good care of you."

When I don't reply, maybe because I'm sort of overcome by these promises that answer basically every wish

I've ever had times around a thousand. More than that. I've never even *thought* to wish for what Rafe is promising me.

"Let's go up on deck and I'll have them bring us some food," he says. "Okay?"

"Okay."

God, I hope I survive this.

15

WE EAT and we swim and then we sit on the deck and watch the sunset.

And Rafe starts asking those questions again.

Holding his hand, high on some perfect cocktail of endorphins and champagne, his questions begin to burrow deeper, like everything else about him has. Rafe, all male energy and buff, pirate perfection, has never looked more dazzling. His black hair touches the sweat-dampened back of his neck in glinting flicks, adding to his rogue appeal.

"Okay, where were we?" He feeds me a strawberry. "You haven't told me what your favorite book is."

"I have a lot of favorite books. That's what happens, I guess, when you spend half your life in libraries. I had a lot of time to read."

'Because..."

"They're quiet. And they were always a lot warmer than—"

He looks over at me. "Warmer than...?"

"My house. We couldn't afford electricity sometimes. It used to get...cold."

He pauses. "We couldn't either. But in Florida, it didn't get cold. It got hot. I used to hate having to read with a weak flashlight all the time, though."

It's a surrender of sorts, admitting these things. We're growing closer. Very slowly, we're beginning to trust.

Even so, Rafe shocks me with his honesty. "My mother died when I was eight. Max was four. He doesn't really remember her. My father was a businessman with interests in both oil and fraud. He made a couple of bad deals and big mistakes that completely ruined him. He killed himself when he lost his fortune. Shot himself with a sawed-off double-barreled shotgun. Very Hemingway. I was ten years old. I found him."

My hand covers my mouth. "Rafe," I finally say. "I'm so sorry."

"We got sent to our uncle's place in Florida," he continues matter-of-factly. "He lived alone. He had a small practically-derelict house with an even smaller cabin out back. Max and I moved in and lived in that cabin for almost seven years. It was on low stilts and when the storms hit, it used to flood us out now and then. But we had nothing worth saving except the clothes on our backs and a couple of surfboards."

The sun is sinking lower now, painting the water a brilliant shade of orange. I barely notice. And Rafe keeps talking. "Our uncle was a lowlife. A real fucking scumbag. A drunk. He worked odd jobs but he didn't have enough money to feed us. So we stole, to begin with. I got a job in a surf shop waxing boards, which I could do after school and on the weekends. I kept Max with me a lot of the time but he was so young. He was a hell-raiser even then. I tried my hardest to keep him out of trouble. The job brought in enough to keep us from going hungry, but only just. Not enough to get the electricity hooked up. Just enough for batteries, so we could read, and I could help Max with his homework. I knew school was our only out. So I was cut-throat about it. I forced myself to succeed. I was blind to everything except the drive of getting us out of there."

"I used to read in the dark, too," I say softly, amazed at our common ground. "By candlelight." He waits, and I can sense that he's eager to hear whatever I'll give him. "My father left, and my mother never recovered from that. She was completely heartbroken, and scared, I guess. All alone with a baby like that. My mother was...broken, I guess. She started drinking and never stopped. She just couldn't cope. It was like he took part of her along with him when he left us. Everything about her just drifted away, or got drowned in that bottle."

I don't really want to keep talking about all the baggage of my depressing childhood. But we're on a roll now. We're taking turns and Rafe's fists are sort of clenched now. "It was only a few weeks into my junior year that I came home after working in the surf shop one day. Max was sitting in the corner with a knife in his hand and our uncle was lying on the floor in a puddle of blood. I'd never seen so much blood. Our uncle had tried to...do something to Max, so Max grabbed a knife and killed the fucker. I thought about taking him and running, but I knew it would ruin our lives even more. I figured they'd have to understand it was self-defense. He ended up spending more than a year locked up in juvie. By the time he got out I'd earned most of a full ride to Stanford. Max stayed in my dorm with me until they figured it out."

Certain things are starting to make sense to me. About Rafe. About his overdeveloped sense of protectiveness. "You spent all these years taking care of him."

"I tried to. Sometimes I think I fucked him up more than I helped him. He might have been better off in foster care. But I just couldn't just hand him over to some stranger who could've been as bad as what we'd escaped from, or even worse. I was all he had. I had to try to make it work. But Max...I still worry about him. He's been in trouble a couple of times. He uses women. He lacks remorse in a way that pisses me off sometimes. He's got a real...dark side. He doesn't think of consequences. And he's still a hell-raiser."

"And you're still helping him."

"Giving him a job is the least I can do for him. He's good at making money when he puts his mind to it. He can charm people easily enough. Too easily, maybe. But there's a piece of him that...I don't know. There's that piece that's always going to be that terrified little kid with a bloody knife in his hands."

"You did the right thing." This is the most personal conversation I've ever had with anyone—ever—about my past. I know without asking that it's equally ground-breaking for Rafe. The last sliver of the sun sinks below the horizon. "Foster care is...not something I would wish on my worst enemy."

Very gently: "You were in foster care?"

It's hard to talk about, but I'm this far in, and Rafe has been honest with me, so I keep going. "Later. My mother's state of mind deteriorated. I spent as much time as I could at school and at the library. Even when I was young, I was determined to do well in school and—like you, I guess—dig my way out of that hole. But then I'd have to go home again."

This next part is harder to talk about, but it feels almost therapeutic. I *want* to tell Rafe. Then I want to forget about it for good. "There was one man in particular who moved in with us for a while. He lived with us about ten years ago, when I was around ten." My voice has become rasped and Rafe's face shows the beginnings of anger. He's anticipating what I was about to say. "He used to threaten me and...well, threaten to do things. It was...as terrifying as it sounds."

Rafe's question is guarded, like he might not be able to deal with the answer. "Did he hurt you?"

"No. But I knew he would if I stayed. So I left, before he could." I realize my face is wet. I hate that memory. "Anyway, he finally left, but by then my mother was too far gone to take care of me, and she died soon after all that happened. I got put into foster care and things got even worse. I ran away a lot."

"Jesus, Lexi. You didn't have anyone else who could have helped you?"

"My father was gone. My mother had passed away. She was an only child and as far as I knew, my grandparents were either dead or didn't know I existed. I was a ward of the state. The foster families they chose for me didn't seem like...good ones. Whenever I felt unsafe, which was basically all the time, I ran away. I hid in the library, sometimes even at night, and other places. But I always went to school. I kept my hiding places close enough to get there. No matter what. And I was pretty good at pretending that everything was fine. I washed my clothes in the river. There was a second hand store with two-dollar jeans and t-shirts. One of my teachers noticed, eventually, when I was almost fourteen, and took a special interest in me. I was put in a foster home with an old woman. It was the nicest house I'd ever lived in. It was warm. And there was food in the fridge. She had an attic and left me to myself. I stayed with her for three years, until I left for college."

"Christ." Rafe's rage is laced by a compassion that's so full of understanding it undoes me a little. It's not the memories that are making me cry. It's not even the relief that my life has changed so profoundly from those horrific, dark days. It's Rafe's *grasp* of my damages that plunges right into my heart like a jagged spear. Releasing all those pent-up secrets that were so scary and painful all those years ago.

Confessing and sharing all that is powerful.

That *he gets it* is even more intense.

His understanding feels like solace.

It feels like trust.

It feels like love.

RAFE WIPES my tears with his fingers. "I'm here now." His voice has gone all husky. "You're safe and you'll never have to worry again."

It's comments like this one that I can't quite fully absorb. *Never* is a long time. Too long to think about.

"I'm just thinking about your timeline. Your mother

died when you were ten. And that was around ten years ago, you said."

"Yes."

"So that would make you...*twenty*?"

"Nicely done, professor. Now I get why you're the CEO."

"Seriously?"

"I'll be twenty-one in a couple of months."

"You graduated early?"

"I skipped seventh grade."

"All that library time," he comments gently.

"Yeah."

"And you? You just had a birthday."

"Twenty-seven."

"Hmm. An older man."

"I'm glad you told me, honey. Everything."

"Me too, Rafe. And I'm glad you told me." It's true. On both fronts. I haven't told him *everything*, but I do feel closer to the elusive Rafe Black than I've ever felt to anyone in my entire life. I don't know what that says about me, or him, and I don't care. All I know is that I'm glad I survived all those dark days and terrifying nights, all that work and struggle and desperation. Because it all brought me to *this* moment, and it's one of such glittering magnificence that, against all odds, it finally feels worth it.

16

———

RAFE

"I'M TAKING you out to dinner tonight." We ended up spending a couple of days on the boat, where I finally began to break through Lexi's barriers. At least I can begin to *try* to understand that reserve in her now, the one that drives me slightly mad because she's holding back from me.

She told me she loves me. The sweetest words I ever heard.

Still, there are details of herself and her past she's protecting. Or hiding. I'm aware of this. But I'll take what I can get for now and work on getting the rest later.

I have never, ever in my life felt this...*desperate*, if that's even the right word for it. To get close to a woman. To know everything about her. To protect her and guard her like a goddamn gladiator. I'm in love. I'm in lust, on steroids. And there's something else...that, I can admit, is almost concerning. I feel like I could kill for her. I *know* I could kill for her. I'm supposed to be a civilized, educated pillar of society, possibly. What I feel like is an obsessed Viking who, if another man so much as *looks* at my girl, wouldn't hesitate to kill the fucker with my bare hands.

Like with everything else about Lexi, this is a first for me. I've never felt jealous before. And I can tell you this much: it's fucking *intense.*

She's lying on the couch, reading a glossy magazine. She's wearing a white bikini and nothing else. Her olive skin is tanned to a light golden color. She has a sprinkling of freckles across her shoulders and the bridge of her nose. I've kissed every one of them. Her hair has been bleached a shade by the sun to a straw-colored white-blond. Her eyebrows and eyelashes are a shade darker than her hair and are, for some reason, fascinating to me. Her lips are one of my favorite things on the planet and her eyes...well, her eyes, that are now watching me watch her, are a light, jewel-like shade of green, sparked with brightness and perceptive humor and a deep, unfathomable...soulfulness. If all of the above wasn't enough, it's that last detail most of all that's wound itself tightly around my heart and gripped it. Painfully. Totally.

I finally understand why they say love hurts.

"Where are we going to go?" she asks. "That resort down the beach?"

"Yes. They have good food. I thought you might like a break from my cooking."

"I like your cooking." She's smiling, and what I really feel like doing is kissing every inch of her, from those eyebrows to those lips, down her unbelievably beautiful breasts, peeling off that tiny bikini so I can taste every sweet—but no. I've already made love to her three times today. I'm learning that I simply can't get enough. My lust doesn't...slake. My cock never *goes down*. The hair, the lips, the eyes, the nipples, and don't even get me started on her perfect pink pussy which is heaven on earth.

I'll wait until after we've had dinner, even though I don't *want* to wait. I also don't want to hound her like a man possessed. Even though that's exactly what I am. "We'll take one of the jet skis. There's a place we can park it at the resort."

She stands up and...*holy fuck*. I don't think I'll ever get used to her beauty. The outer beauty, which is pretty much like a punch to the gut every time I look at her. And the inner beauty, that shines out of those green eyes and makes me want to know her and get closer to her and be the one she wants to be with every minute of every day.

Yes, it's a problem how completely fucking hooked I am, but I'm dealing with it.

"Can I drive?" She smiles.

"No. I'll drive."

She blinks those long eyelashes at me and twirls a strand of that long, sunny hair.

I want to drive. To make sure she's safe. "I think I should drive, honey. Do you even know how to ride a jet ski?"

"You can teach me." She stands up on her toes and leans that absurdly gorgeous body against mine. Then she kisses me lightly with *those lips. God help me.* "Please, Rafey?"

Fuck. Of course I'll give her anything she wants. "You can sit in front of me and I'll show you how. But I get to steer."

"*I* want to steer." Another kiss. This time she parts her lips and I sink my tongue into her mouth lustily because I can't help myself. I'm light-headed because she tastes so damn good.

"If we end up getting wet, I'm blaming it on you."

She laughs, then skips out the door to get her little white dress, which is out by the hot tub where she left it earlier. I find a shirt and follow her, cursing the perpetual monster hard-on in my shorts that's showing no sign of deflating. I'm wondering how I'm going to handle being in public with her.

How did this happen to me?

I'm almost nostalgic for the good old days, when I didn't *feel* emotion, or give a fuck about anyone but myself and Max. When life was simple and I wasn't mired in a total haze of raging lust and insanity-edged obsession.

How did this unassuming little nymphet plow into my life like a category five hurricane and completely obliterate my control?

I launch the jet ski and help Lexi onto it, then I sit behind her, wrapping my arms around her. I fire up the engine and show her how to ease the throttle higher, which she does—much too fast—causing us to lurch into warp speed. It's amazing to me that my first instinct is to protect her. My arm wraps around her as I grab for the throttle, steadying the jet ski's balance—just a little too late.

We tip. And both fall into the water.

I'm still holding on to her. We surface and she's laughing. A full-on laugh like this is the funniest thing that's ever happened. I think my heart might literally be melting. The squirming wetness of her body in my arms and her laughter, which is so infectious I find *myself* laughing—which I don't do often enough, come to think of it—is killing me.

God, I'm so fucking in *love* with her.

I kiss her but she can't even kiss me back because she's laughing so hard. "Sorry, Rafe," she says sweetly, fingering a strand of my hair.

"Can I drive now?"

"No."

"No?"

"I won't tip us again, I promise."

I hesitate, but when she kisses me, I give in, like the utterly-whipped softie (in every way except one) I've become.

I grab the jet ski and boost her back up on to it before climbing on behind her. I place my hand over hers to help her ease the jet ski forward without catapulting us overboard and she gets the hang of it this time.

We get to the resort without toppling off again and the warm breeze dries our clothes, at least partly. I'm kind of regretting this now. Her little white sundress is damp and practically see-through, clinging to the her ludicrously-nubile body. The tiny bikini underneath doesn't leave much to the imagination. At all.

People can see her. *Other* people.

This is surprisingly unacceptable to me. But she's already walking down the dock.

The place is crowded for happy hour. All the people staying at the resort are on vacation time and have probably been drinking all day. There's a lot of laughter and live music from a band playing from a small raised stage in the corner. Daylight is just beginning to fade and there are strings of lights hung around the bar, giving the whole place a festive feel.

I tie up the jet ski and we make our way toward the bar, which is packed.

I keep my arm slung firmly around Lexi.

They know me here. A hostess comes up and offers to show us to a table, even though they're probably fully booked. "Two for dinner, Mr. Black? Your usual table?"

"Yes. Thank you."

"Just give me a minute to get it set up. Can I offer you a drink while you wait?"

"A bottle of Bollinger on ice and two glasses."

"Right away, Mr. Black."

The hostess disappears and Lexi glances up at me, with that look on her face—the one she gives me when she thinks I'm being arrogant or overly bossy. "You have a special table they set up just for you?"

"I give good tips."

"Mr. Black always gets what he wants," she says, chiding me, maybe.

"Mr. Black isn't getting what he wants right *now*. So the answer to that would be no." I slide my hand down to her ass, in case she doesn't fully grasp what I mean and she smiles but she shimmies away from me, which is probably a good thing, since my hard-on is already obvious and it's only gaining momentum.

"I'm just going to find the ladies room," Lexi says. "I'll be right back."

"It's through that door right there." But I don't like the idea of her wandering around...alone.

Christ, yet a grip, man. What the fuck are you going to do, follow her in there?

The hostess is back. "Your table is ready, Mr. Black."

"I'll meet you at the table," Lexi says, and then she's walking away, through the crowd, and I feel almost stricken with panic. My protective urges are on overdrive and they're so voracious they're practically unbearable. Watching her walk away...I'm really not sure I can deal with this.

For fuck's sake, Rafe. Go to your table and have a drink. What are you, a fucking stalker now? Calm the fuck down.

Yes. Yes. That's what I need to do.

I can do that.

She'll be back in five minutes. Everything's fine.

So I do. I walk over to the table, which is on a raised deck overlooking the water in a private little hut-like area that has a good view of both the beach and the pool. The waitress has set down two menus and is pouring the champagne.

I thank her as she walks away and take a sip of my drink.

Stay calm.

Don't make a scene.

Absolutely do not walk inside to make sure she's okay.

This is ridiculous. I've morphed into a raving lunatic.

And then I see her. The flashy light of her flaxen hair.

She's making her way through the crowd, which has gotten rowdier even in the last ten minutes. The music's louder.

God, she's stunning.

Is she this beautiful to everyone, or just to me? I have no way of knowing.

And then...she stops. Someone's talking to her. A man. *Two* men. They say something to her and she smiles and tries to keep walking. But then *one of them grabs her arm*, not aggressively, but as though playfully. To keep her there.

I didn't think the expression "to see red" was actually a thing until right now. I literally *do* see red. My blood feels like it's boiling. My heart is beating fast and my muscles are coiled and unbelievably tense. I'm pushing my way through the crowd and people are pissed off but I hardly notice them. I grab the shirt of the guy who's holding Lexi's arm with my fist and shove him up against the wall. Some glasses shatter and people are reacting. The only thing I'm aware of is this asshole who *touched* her. I have him in a stranglehold against the wall and I'm about to punch his face.

"*Rafe!*" Lexi is trying to pull me off. "*Rafe, stop!*"

"Jeez, man, what the fuck?" the guy is saying. "What'd I *do*?"

My voice sounds cold when I speak, like the voice of someone else. "If you ever even *think* about touching this girl again, I'll tell you what's going to happen. I'm going to beat you—and your friend here—to a fucking bloody pulp, do you hear me?"

"What'd *I* do?" the other guy says.

I'm still looking directly into the eyes of the prick that grabbed Lexi's arm. "Do you understand what I'm telling you? Or do I need to pummel some goddamn understanding into your pea-sized brain to make entirely sure you *do* fucking understand what I'm telling you?" I seriously don't know where this is coming from. I've never been much of a fighter. I used to go out of my way to *avoid* conflict. Until now. My fist is actually *craving* a good, solid punch right in the middle of this guy's idiotic face.

But Lexi's pulling at my arm. "*Rafe.* Stop this right now! Come on. Let's go to our table. *Stop*, Rafe. I mean it."

For her, I do, and because the guy is clearly scared shitless of me. I don't blame him. I could kill, and if the need arises, I *will* kill. He seems to be able to read this in my eyes.

Jesus. It's hardly a reason to kill someone, you psycho. But it's no use. My subconscious is no match for my inner caveman.

"I didn't even know she was with anyone, dude," the punk says.

"Well, now you do."

"Okay. *Okay.* Calm down, man."

I'm about as far from calm as I've ever been.

"Rafe. Seriously. This is crazy." Lexi's still pulling my arm and I finally relent and let the guy go.

He glares at me, straightening his shirt and sidling away, along with his friend.

If anything, I feel even more worked up than ever, as Lexi pulls me by the hand and we walk to our table. The entire restaurant is staring at us but I honestly don't give a fuck. "Let's go back to the house," I say.

"We'll have dinner, Rafe. Then we'll go back. You're acting crazy. What *was* that? What's gotten in to you?"

Hmm, let me think about that, Lexi. Somewhere over the course of the past week and a half, I've become addicted to you on a scale that might be described as manic, unhealthy and possibly even destructive. And I don't know exactly how to handle it.

"Come on," she says. "We'll have a drink and some food and then we'll go back. You can drive us back. Everything's fine."

Is it fine? Is it?

We sit our table and she hands me my glass of champagne and I chug the whole goddamn thing. Lexi's staring at me like she's worried. And so she should be.

17

I OPEN MY EYES. It's early morning and I'm lying naked under the plush quilted duvets of Rafe's bed. My hand roves to search the cool, unoccupied other half.

"Rafe?" I sit up, and the covers fall to my waist. We're back in L.A.

He's sitting in a leather chair next to the floor-to-ceiling windows, dressed only in worn jeans. His feet are propped onto a zebra-patterned ottoman. His MacBook is perched on his lap. He's deeply tanned and the tips of his black hair are a shade lighter, bleached by the Hawaiian sun. The disheveled state of his hair, the bronze of his muscular, hair-dusted chest and the safari-themed furniture make him look rugged and edgy. I break his concentration, and he looks up. His eyes study my face, my mussed-up hair, my naked breasts. His expression is laced with that lazy arrogance that's equal parts annoyingly cocky and sexy as hell. A stranger might find his expression unapproachable, almost cold. I know better. "Hi," I say.

"Hey, baby," he says. "Look on the nightstand. I got you a present."

A small gift has been wrapped in gold paper. I keep telling him not to buy me things but he never listens.

"Open it."

I do, and it's the latest iPhone. He couldn't believe I'm still using the 4S I bought second-hand when I was a freshman.

"I sent you a text," he says. I touch the screen and it comes up.

XOXO I LOVE YOU

Two weeks in Hawaii has bonded me to Rafe irrevocably. I'm not going to say our relationship is...easy. It's definitely the most intense thing that's ever happened to me, by a scale of around a million to one. I worry a little about *how* intense it is. Our connection was forged by a white-hot lust that has deepened into something else altogether. We've both said the L word. I said it once. He's said it five times. Now six. Not that I'm counting, but I haven't heard those three little words in a very long time, and that was different. So it's memorable. And kind of huge.

Somewhere under all that need and beauty and comfort is the smallest thread, though, of something else.

A feeling of being consumed in the fire. I've thought of bringing it up with Rafe, to let him know that I'm going to need a little bit of space once in a while so I can...not lose myself completely. But then he'll say something sweet or do something thoughtful, like this, or drive me wild with his passion, and it passes.

Besides, if I'm being honest with myself, I'm as possessive of him as he is of me. His jealousy at the resort shocked me, of course it did. The way he reacted was unexpected. It was also...*hot*. Maybe it shouldn't have been. Maybe I should have demanded to jump on the next flight out. But, after my early years—the sense of being abandoned and neglected in one way or another by everyone in my life who was supposed to care about me—there's something wildly comforting about being cared about *that* damn much. Some small part of me *loves* that he's so intense about it.

So it's not just him. It's both of us. Our bond is complicated, just like everyone else's probably is.

"Thank you, Rafe. You didn't need to—"

"I want to be able to keep in touch with you whenever I need to. This one's more reliable."

It's so...*swish* and modern. I'm sure it'll take me a while to figure out all the new apps he's pre-loaded it with. I set the phone down on the nightstand. "You're working?"

After the uninterrupted hedonism of Kauai, I'm used to his undivided attention. To having him all to myself. The minute we cleared the LAX runway yesterday evening, he started stealing moments to check emails and read reports.

I don't mind.

Of course he needs to do all that. Last night I was happy enough to catch up on some sleep and leave him to it, but now, I'm well-rested. And he looks too delicious. All those burnished muscles and shadowed stubble.

Rafe pauses before giving me an oblique reply. "I've been away for two weeks."

"I know." I can hear the churlishness in my voice. He hears it too and his mouth twitches as he stares at me. Then his attention returns to his computer screen.

It's been a topic we've been avoiding. I tried to bring it up once or twice when we first arrived in Hawaii, then again on the last day of our trip. Both times, he dismissed my question, changing the subject. I quietly agreed: it hadn't been the time or place to talk about work. We could figure out the details once we finally returned to reality.

But now, here it is. Reality is upon us. It's shining its blue light onto the planes of Rafe's sculpted chest, flickering its insistence across his perfect face. For some reason, this makes me feel uneasy.

I lay back into the nest of Rafe's bed, displacing the covers in the process. I stretch lightly, completely aware that Rafe is now watching me. I rise from the bed. The carpet is soft and cushioned under my feet. I pad over to him as he watches me, closely circling his chair as I coil a finger through the coarse silk of his hair. "What day is it?"

"Saturday."

"Your work can't wait until Monday?"

"There are a couple of issues at Max's company that need attention." There's a curtness in his tone that's new. He's conflicted. Pressing concerns at his companies have been cast aside for me, for two whole weeks. I know this is unprecedented. Which is flattering, sure, that he's as changed by me as I am by him.

Still, there's something not quite...*even* about the fact that he has a life outside of *us*. And I don't. I have Tess, and that's pretty much it. And I have this job. If Rafe will *let* me have this job, that is.

And even though I'm not thrilled by the turn of my own thoughts, I also feel weirdly possessive of him. I'm too used to owning his time completely. It's all I've ever known of him and I'm surprised at how hard it is to give him up, even for a few hours.

Besides, if I am going to be his assistant, he could start showing me the ropes a little.

"So we're working today?" I know it's a touchy subject, so I do my best to introduce it as casually as possible.

His dark blue eyes show no emotion aside from a simmering, controlled lust. "*We're* not working today, no. *I'm* catching up on a few emails today, and I might spend a few hours in my office this afternoon. *You're* relaxing. And tonight, we can go out somewhere if you want."

"I don't need to relax. I've relaxed more in the past two weeks than I ever have in my life." It's true, depending on how you define relaxation. A lot of it was relaxation of the strenuous and somewhat kinky variety. Either way, my frustrations are on a roll. "When do you want me to start helping you?"

Here I am, naked and mussed-up from sleep and a sexual marathon that's as energetic on the fifteenth day as it was on the first. I'm too satiated to be frenzied about it, but my desire for Rafe is so ingrained in me by this point that just touching his hair is enough to kick-start the gentle pulse, the secret heat. I think about taking his laptop and setting it aside, unzipping his jeans, climbing onto him and straddling his hips. Working him. Taking his hardening length into my hands. My mouth. Insisting that he give me everything. But I'm irked by the way his eyes keep glancing at the screen. And his dismissive tone is pissing me off. Maybe I *already* started working, at my job interview. Maybe *this* is all he intends for me to do: to service his whims when he's in the mood. I know enough about his body language to read his distraction.

Fine.

I grab one of his shirts that's draped over a chair. A white button-down made of thick, expensive cotton. I wrap it around myself and it hangs to the tops of my thighs. I sit on the couch next to his chair. I might be overreacting a *tiny* bit when I say, "Would you like me to take some notes for you, boss? You've only put half my skills to good use so far."

He looks at me, and his annoyance gives way to a light, exhaled laugh. "Come on, Lexi. Don't get all petulant over a couple of emails."

"I'm not petulant." Petulantly, yes. For good reason.

I'm almost hyper-aware of my jealousy, or whatever this is. Maybe because I gave up almost every detail of my pre-Rafe life at the drop of a hat for him, as soon as he'd snapped his fingers. I was ridiculously willing to step into his world and leave all of mine behind.

Too willing, maybe.

Rafe gets to keep everything. He gets to run his companies and live in his apartment and have dinner with his brother and his employees. He doesn't have to give up anything because all the good stuff is his. His business and apartment and money. His jets and chefs and beach houses and yachts.

All I have is him. And Tess, but she's got her own life, her own business and last time I talked to her she'd even been out on a couple of dates with a new guy she met at a party.

In Hawaii it was only us. Back here in L.A., the scales between me and Rafe feel uneven. Not only that, but the creeping suspicion that he no longer wants me to work for him is becoming more and more obvious. He still hasn't answered my question. His attention is once again diverted to his computer.

"Rafe?"

"Hmm?" Typing.

"Have you changed your mind?"

"About what?"

"About hiring me."

He types a few more words. Then he leans back in his chair and folds his arms across his chest. It's several seconds before he speaks. "I've been thinking."

I have a feeling I know exactly what he's been thinking about. "You have?"

He balks, cagily avoiding the topic. "There's a private gym on the tenth floor."

"So?"

He laughs again. "There's a pool outside. A jacuzzi. I'm sure you can keep yourself busy for half an hour while I answer a couple of emails."

"You didn't answer my question."

"It's just emails. This isn't the kind of stuff you can help me with at this point. It won't take long. An hour at the most. Then I'll take you out, wherever you want to go."

"I'll tell you what," I start pulling on the short skirt I'd worn the day before. I button the middle two buttons of his shirt and tie the front into a knot to create a half-shirt that reveals the skin of my stomach. "I might go and get some fresh air. Since you're busy. I'm going to call Tess and meet up with her. I've been a terrible friend." I've called her every couple of days, but she's dying for more detail. Suddenly, I miss her terribly. I need to talk to someone who isn't...Rafe. "We can meet back here later on. Or we can meet at a restaurant, for dinner. Tell me which one and I'll see you there at...how's seven? Or would eight be better?" I pull on my pair of (yes, Balenciaga) boots.

It's true that in all the time I've known Rafe, he's basically never let me out of his sight. But of course this is a scenario that can't sustain itself. He can hardly follow me around like a jumped-up bodyguard now that we're back to our lives and work schedules.

Rafe's expression darkens and he's no longer looking at his computer screen.

I keep my tone light. "That way you can catch up on everything you need to do."

"No."

"No? No, you don't want to meet up back here? Or no, you don't want to go to dinner?"

"I want you to stay here."

I don't feel at all proud of the small surge of triumph, but I know I've gotten to him. "As long as you're working, and you don't need me, I might as well go spend some time with Tess. I know she's dying to hear about Hawaii—"

"I said no."

I let his comment hang in the air, ignoring it as I

put on some pink lipstick. I lean toward the mirror. I can practically feel the heat of his gaze on me as I move. Then I put on some mascara—make-up that Rafe bought me on Rodeo Drive, at ridiculous expense—and unbutton the top button of the shirt I'm wearing, to spritz a spray of perfume. I'm not wearing anything underneath my clothes, a detail he's obviously aware of.

He can be as stubborn and overbearing as he wants, but he can't actually stop me from going out. Besides, this whole topic of am-I-going-to-be-his-assistant-or-aren't-I is getting tedious. He's being so frustratingly noncommittal about it and I need a break. And I really *do* want to see Tess. We have a lot to talk about.

I ignore my dread at the thought of leaving him. He's come to feel like part of me, after the intense connectivity we've shared. I'm so in love with him it scares me. Even if he is acting like an over-controlling jerk at this precise moment.

The air feels sparked with a charged volatility.

I grab my new Chanel handbag. "Let me know what you decide," I say, heading toward the door of his bedroom.

Rafe looks almost comically appalled. Then his disbelief turns to something else altogether. Fury. He practically drops his laptop as he stands, striding over to me to block my path. He wraps his arm around my waist, not painfully, but with undeniable force. "Lexi," he says softly. "You're not going out like that."

"Like what?"

"Like...that," he says.

I pull away from him. After his remorse over being rough with me, he's mostly been more gentle. But there are still occasional bruises on my skin from his punishing grip during sex. These tend to drive him crazy. "I'm going out, Rafe. Let go of me."

He does let go, but now his palm is on the door, blocking my escape. "Lexi. Please." I know this is him being protective, but I don't need his protection right now. What I need is for him to let me out. "Come on," he whispers, half threat, half plead. "Stay."

"It's only for a few hours. You said it yourself. You want to work and you don't need my help. That's cool. I get it. I'll see you when you're finished answering your emails. We can talk about the rest of it later."

Both his hands are on me now, snaking around me. He pulls me against him in a hug that's too strong. I can feel his power and his desperation in the flex of his muscles and the beat of his heart. "Don't go."

"Rafe. What is this? You won't even notice I'm gone. You'll be busy. You can talk to Max and solve whatever problems have come up. Call me in a few hours and tell me where to meet you."

His lips brush against my hair as he holds me close.

His hands are moving lower, his grip very nearly painful. "I can call Max later. I don't want you out there, alone."

"*Rafe.* This is crazy. I'll be fine. Let me go. I want to. You have to let me go."

But he's pulling up the hem of my skirt. His overblown control, for the very first time, feels constricting. His palms slide possessively over the rounded curves of my ass, pulling me against his big, hard body. His fingers explore, sliding into the damp hollow between my legs, finding the slippery heat. "You're wet for me." His breathing has grown heavier. "You want me."

"I'm not," I protest. But of course I am. I *am* wet. The minute I opened my eyes to the shine of his hair and the masculine contours of his shoulders, I felt the stirring warmth, which is never hard to summon in Rafe's presence. But I need some space from his commands. I'm still angry at him for his indecision about whether or not he wants to hire me. I don't blame him for not being sure about it, after everything that's happened. He might be trying to let me down easy. Maybe he's considering reassigning me. Or maybe somewhere along the lines his plans for me have changed.

Either way, I need some space.

My own control—over everything—is slipping. I've already become too dependent on him. And I can't breathe.

Stepping back from him, I feel his knuckles slide intimately. I gasp as I disengage from him, pulling at the hem of my skirt. I'm confused and disarmed by the swell of emotion. This should have been easy, this raging torrent of attraction. But the deeper into it we get, the more complicated it feels. Mindless attraction was only the beginning. Somewhere along the way, this relationship has drifted into darker, swifter, more complex waters. "Stop," I tell him. "Let me go."

Rafe's face is heart-breaking to me. He's hurt and angered by my refusal. I turn away from him. I don't want to see him. Like always, he's unsettling me with his beauty. I need some distance. I need to *not* break down or give in. "I said I'm going out. I need to be alone for a while. I'll call you later." I reach for the bag I dropped somewhere in the middle of our tryst.

But Rafe leans against the door, blocking me in. "There's no need for you to go out right now. You can be alone all you want, here. You can invite Tess over for lunch. Bennett will cook you anything you want."

My heart is pounding, with some crazy cocktail of rage, lust and fear. I know he's controlling, I'd known it all along. Maybe I underestimated the extent of it.

How far will he go to stop me?

He remains motionless, his eyes darker than I've ever seen them. I stand in front of him, but I don't touch him. I'm not afraid of violence. I'm afraid touching him will undermine my resolve. Despite being furious with him, I *know* touching him will undermine my resolve.

"Rafe, you can't *keep* me here. I'm free to go whenever and wherever I want. I'm not your goddamn prisoner!"

"Just give me twenty minutes," he says. "Then we'll sit in the hot tub together. Or go shopping. Or out to lunch. Whatever you want."

"What I *want* is for you to move away from that door and let me out!" His behavior is unacceptable, that's all there is to it. "You can't *force* me to stay holed up in this apartment and never leave! Seriously, who does that? You're acting like some kind of lunatic."

Rafe doesn't move from the door. He reaches to touch an end strand of my hair. He coils a tangled curl. "I'm not *forcing* you to do anything. I'm *asking* you to stay with me." With one finger, he touches my chin and tilts my face up to his. "Please, Lexi. Don't walk out on me." His voice is soothingly deep, crooning to me like *I'm* the psycho, or some wild animal about to bolt. "Stay with me, baby girl. I'll do whatever you want. Anything."

"Okay, then do this: *move*, out of my way. You don't want me to start my new job today. You don't even want to *talk* to me about whether or not I'll be starting my new job, ever, so there's really nothing else to discuss right now."

A loaded pause. "I was thinking that...after all that's happened, and considering the nature of our relationship, as it's turned out, that maybe we might want to...re-evaluate your position. The thing is, Lexi, you don't really *have* to work. At all. Not now."

I can't believe this. "You're *firing* me?"

"No, I'm not *firing* you. I'm telling you that I—"

"That you don't want me to work for you anymore." Bastard!

"Only because we're in a relationship now, Lex. Things have changed. I'm not sure if it's a good idea."

I'm too pissed off to listen to this. "Oh, that's just *great*. Let me get this straight. You won't let me out of this fucking apartment and now you don't want me to work. You want to keep me locked up here in your bedroom to *fuck* me whenever you feel like it. If I'm actually *working* and doing something productive, engaging my mind, using my degree that cost the every ounce of blood, sweat and tears I had, not to mention costing the goddamn *earth*, which will take me a million years to pay off, I might not be available when you want me. Your hard-on might go unaddressed for half an hour while I go have coffee with a friend or finish typing up one of your reports. I might have to *talk* to people. Or use my brain instead of just my body. You'd just hate *that*, wouldn't you, Rafe?"

He's staring at me, aggressively. He's hurt. "Lexi. That's not what I fucking meant. I'm telling you that there's no longer a need for you to earn money. I'll take care of it. I'll pay off your student loan and pay for anything else you need. I'll take care of you."

"What if I don't *want* you to take care of me? What if I want to take care of *myself*? Or what if *I* want to take care of *you*? Did you ever think of *that*?"

He looks a little stunned by my reply, like he hasn't, in fact, thought of anything like that before.

And I'm too furious to wait for his answer. "*Fine*, Rafe. Go ahead and fire me. If that's what you really want to do, just do it! And I'll tell you what *I* really want to do: *get out of here*. I've got some job-hunting to do. Because the thing is, I *want* to work. I *like* working. And I need some fresh air. So please get out of my way so I can get started."

"Lexi, for fuck's sake—"

He reaches for my hand but I shake him off. "And I've changed my mind about dinner. I don't want to eat with you tonight. I'm going out with friends. I'm going to stay with Tess tonight."

I don't mention that the only friend I have in L.A. is probably working or has already made other plans.

Rafe stands there, like a big, stubborn brick wall. From the place where he dropped it by the window, his computer pings with a new email message alert. "Go on," I say. "Answer your emails. Don't let me stop you."

"Lexi. Be reasonable. There's no need to get all fucking crazy on me. I'm asking you to let me take care of you, and to stay. It's hardly cruel and unusual punishment. We can talk about this."

"Of course we can. Later."

There's something not at all right about the submission he demands of me. I'm trapped. And now I'm going to be rendered useless, except for one purpose. He can placate me with calm requests, but it's not enough. "Get out of my way, Rafe."

"I'm not letting you leave like this, Lexi. Let's sit down and—"

"I don't want to sit down! And it's not up to you to *let* me do anything! *Get out of my way, Rafe. I mean it!*" I push at his shoulder in an attempt to move him but he's probably twice my weight and a good six inches taller, not to mention strong as a goddamn ox.

"*Lexi*," he growls, in a futile attempt to stop me, and calm me. His arms wrap around me in a stronghold, not forcefully, but with extreme, absolute strength. I'm struggling, fighting him, pushing against him, but his hold is unbreakable. He slides down to a sitting position, cradling my squirming, writhing, uncontrolled body in his lap, forming a cage with his muscular arms and legs. I might be crying in my frustration because what he's doing is wrong but it's also wildly comforting, even if it is a prison of sorts. I *want* him to want me like this. Obsessively. Possessively. I love him too much. I want to break free and at the same time crawl into his body and soul and live there forever.

He's wiping my tears, holding my wrists in one of his fists to stop me from lashing out. He's kissing my face and my lips as he whispers a litany of calming, soothing promises. "You're all right, sweet girl. Of course you can go anywhere you want. I'll come with you. I love you, did you know that? Do you know how much I love you? I can't fucking see straight I love you so much. I can't bear the thought of you walking out that door and onto those streets full of back alleys and predators. I want to protect you so much, Lex. I want to keep you safe. I want to do everything for you, baby. Come on, you're all right. Don't cry. Everything's okay. I've got you."

Rafe's fingers slide over a *very* sensitive place.

Damn him with his low voice and his thick black hair, curling gently around his ears, flicking in uneven strands. And his face, all remorseful. His body, hard and gloriously sculpted, with his jeans low on his hips, unbuttoned, revealing the tantalizing arrow line of dark hair and the gigantic hard ridge.

No.

I deny my urges.

I don't *want* them to, but his words and his scent and his strength are drugging me, an exotic elixir that leeches warmth into my heart, thawing my rage, turning it into something else altogether.

Against every ounce of my better judgement, I let him kiss my parted lips in supplicating little nips that grow deeper, longer. His tongue touches mine gently at first, licking into my mouth. His kiss is soft yet firm, demanding. Rafe is completely in charge, as always, convincing me with his perfect allure that I need him, that I want him beyond reason. The lick of his tongue is feeding tiny darts of pleasure into me, to the tips of my breasts and the dewy, softening heat between my thighs. My skirt has ridden up during our tussle, barely concealing me, and I'm sitting on the half-open button fly of his jeans. The hard textures of the straining denim and the cold buttons against my sensitive flesh make me gasp into his mouth.

"That's my girl," he croons. "See? I can make it up to you, baby. You're so beautiful. I love you so much. You taste so fucking good. Come on, that's it. Let me hold you. Let me kiss you."

Damn him.

I'm writhing now for an entirely different reason, in gentle, circling grinds. He released my hands and I realize one of my fists is entwined in his hair, the other pressed against his chest, sliding lower, down his flat, muscled stomach. To the buttons of his jeans, which I push open blindly as I suck on his tongue.

He maneuvers us, pushing his jeans lower to release himself. My rage has transformed into a flaring, white-hot need. I climb onto him, straddling his hips, grasping and working him, rubbing myself against the massive hardness of him.

I'm still furious at him, and my fury at this point is expressing itself as greed. For pleasure. *My* pleasure.

He unbuttons the shirt I'm wearing and fingers my

nipples, twirling and pulling them into tight peaks as his slippery kisses grow hungrier. The pinching pain delivered by his fingers sends ripples of sweet heat to my fluttering core. I want him there. I want to ride him and fuck him.

I'm not gentle as I guide the slick head of his cock, using him to caress my clit in pressing, rhythmic glides. As determined as I am to give myself pleasure, I can tell that my selfish fever is turning him on beyond belief. His chest rises and falls with heavy breaths. I impale myself by slippery, star-studded degrees, moistening his length with the wetness of my own desire to take more of him.

"*Fuck, yes, baby,*" he groans. "*Use me. Take me. I'm yours. I'm so yours. Everything. All of me.*" I slide down the full length of him until he's fully inside me.

I'm in control now. I rub my breasts against the hair-roughened surface of his chest. I kiss and bite his lips. I ride him, sliding along his rigid length, arching and torturing him with wiggling teases, squeezing him to pull him deeper. As I do, he watches my face, his blue eyes half-drowsed and half-feral with pleasure.

"You're a bully," I whisper, as I squeeze myself around his thick cock. "You can't *control* me, Rafe. You don't *own* me."

He groans again. "I know I don't own you. But I *love* you. It's only because I love you so much. Too much. It's too much."

Goddamn him.

"I'll let you come with me when I go out, this time," I tell him, biting gently into the soft flesh of his lower lip. "On one condition. I get to keep my job. I want to work with you and be with you. And sometimes, when I feel like it, I'm going to use you, like you use me. And I'm going to make love to you wherever and whenever I want."

I don't know if there's anything healthy about the way this is playing out, but I don't care. I love him. I hate him a little too sometimes, like right now. Because I want him so much. Even though what I should be doing is walking straight out the door.

I know he's about to come. So I rise up until he slips from the warm, wet embrace of my body. To punish him. Or something.

To this, Rafe reacts. With practically inhuman strength, he lifts me and lays me onto my back in a move that's as gentle and controlled as it is uncompromising. Laying himself onto me, he enters me aggressively, pushing his big cock as deep as I can take him. "*Mine*," he growls. "Do you hear me, baby girl? You're *mine*." Then he bites my earlobe, whispering into my ear. "You'll let me indulge my obsession, and protect you as I want. And I'll agree to *try* to employ you. I can't guarantee that this will work for me, though. You make me too crazy. I need to be able to focus on my companies, without distractions. And you, my little Lexi, are more of a distraction than I can fucking handle."

He thrusts again, as though to illustrate a point. His

hands are on my ass, holding me in squeezing handfuls as he drives into me, ensuring complete possession. His fingers work me from behind, spreading me and pressing into the secret pucker as his driving plunges find sweet, slick friction inside me. He's relentless. Delicious agony gives way to a climbing, tense beauty. The pumping glide of Rafe's hot cock forces the pleasure higher in heavy, potent bursts.

My climax begins as a high peak of accumulating ecstasy that holds in a feverish swell. Then the pleasure erupts into a wild torrent of clenching spasms that milk Rafe's orgasm from his body in hot pulses. He groans with his release, a low, tortured growl against my neck. Then he goes still and heavy, his cock pulsing out the last gushes of his release deep inside me.

After, we lay still for a while, letting the rush mellow. Physically, we're profoundly connected. And it goes deeper than that. I feel Rafe to the core of my being. I feel every ounce of his weight and his need, which warm me to the depths of my soul. To feel him like this, protective yet conquered, our arms and legs entwined, our hair tangled, the slickness of our lovemaking like a life-giving bond, I can almost forgive him. His overbearing dominance. His over-protectiveness. I can see that his faults are all about his love for me and his desire to keep me close. I understand why he acts the way he does, and I know why he worries. From inside the scope of my own vulnerabilities, I don't just accept his shielding, compulsive tactics, I *crave* them. We can argue about his obsession and his way of handling it, but here and now, with his big, male body on me and in me, in a haze of post-coital bliss, all I can feel is my love for him. My devotion. He's everywhere and everything.

He stirs, levering his weight with his arms. "I'm crushing you," he murmurs, staring into my eyes. "God, how I adore you. I want to live inside you, just like this." He pushes his barely-softened shaft deeper into me, kissing me again in leisurely, lusty bites and licks.

At that moment, his email alert pings and my stomach makes a little growling sound. I thought he might be distracted again by the call of his work, but instead he says, "You're hungry."

I gaze up at him.

"What's it to be? Chocolate cake again? I know it's your favorite. Or something more substantial. I'll get Bennett to make us some brunch. I'll feed you, then we'll see about some of that work. And then we can go meet Tess and I'll leave you to it for a while if you want, then we'll get dinner somewhere nice. Okay?"

"Okay, Rafe." He's telling me what I want to hear, and I can't be angry at him for that. Well, I *can*, but I'm too drawn to the mesmerized adoration in his eyes.

His seraphic face lights up. "Great. See? Everything's fine."

Rafe pulls himself from my body. He lifts me up and carries me to his bed, setting me onto the cool sheets and fluffing the pillows before arranging me against them. Then he leans down to kiss my nipple. One, then the other. I feel suddenly tired, like I often do after multiple earth-shattering orgasms. The Rafe Effect.

"I'll be right back," he says, adding, "I'm going to go grab a few things from the kitchen. Don't go anywhere."

"Ha ha."

This is bad, of course. But I'm worn out, for now.

Rafe smiles pulls up his jeans and buttons them. Then he walks to the door, opening it and disappearing, closing the door behind him.

So here I am.

Wondering what "leave you to it" means. Will he sit in the limo while Tess and I drink our coffee? Will he let me out of his sight? I could ask, but it'll only reignite our argument. He's agreed to let me help him, even if it's a vague offer clearly meant to placate me. Until then, apparently I've given in to this demands. His bullyish, overbearing alpha male requests are totally over the top, half the time. The other half, they're exactly what I want and need.

I can blame him for everything but the truth is, I'm as obsessed as he is.

Our first argument, and we've weathered it mostly unscathed.

While I wait for him, I listen to chirp of his computer.

Should I feel happy? That I won? That he's paying attention to me instead of them?

I don't know.

At least he agreed to *try* to work with me. I'll get to watch him at his game, emperor of the empire, and be with him during the days as well as the nights. The work itself is exciting to me, but even more, I'm relieved that Rafe is letting me in. I want him to trust me and to trust himself.

I only hope he can.

18

RAFE

MAX IS GETTING IMPATIENT, like they all are. He'll have to wait, at least for another hour or two. My priorities haven't exactly changed. It's more like they'd been blown out of the fucking water. I checked in from time to time, made a few critical phone calls. I've been building these systems for seven years. I chose and trained my staff carefully, for good reason. I should be able to take a week or two off if I fucking feel like it, and not have the whole goddamn thing crumble to the ground in ruins. I slogged away for years to make sure my interests had solid foundations and impeccable records.

But there are always glitches. Max is good at his job but my brother is a rebel and always has been. It's part of the reason I gave him a job and put him in charge of his own company. That way, at least I can keep an eye on him and get him out of trouble when he needs me to. He's a punk who doesn't follow rules, inside the boardroom or out of it. His style is reckless, I know that only too well. It's true that sometimes a dose of recklessness works in business. Sometimes it gives you an edge. This time it backfired. The insider-trading fiasco at his company is coming to a head. It's time for me to step in and appease the authorities with solid numbers, with rolling heads and, if necessary, with money.

My nubile nymph wants a slice of the action, and as far as I'm concerned she can have anything she wants. I'm in so deep, I would have appointed her CEO of the fucking company if she made the request into a particularly sublime donut-hold of opportunity. I want her with me. But I also know things can get very complicated very quickly with Lexi around. My total attention is hers whenever she happens to flick me a sultry glance. Or whisper a pouting little command. Or scald me with the shimmery light touch of her fingertips. In the office, that kind of thing could be downright dangerous. Ruinous, even.

I don't trust myself, that's all there is to it. I lose my head on a regular basis with her near me. But the thought of her *not* near me is even worse. It's a problem I'm dealing with.

Bennett's my chef who works on the weekends. He's made breakfast and I take the tray filled with food upstairs.

I get back to my bedroom and find her asleep. I put the covered tray on a table so she can eat when she wakes.

For a few minutes, I just watch her.

She's on the bed where I left her, curled slightly on her side in the sun, her honey-blond hair a cascade of spun gold. She has the power to stun me and energize me at the same time. Love and lust entwined. Who knew the effect could be this potent.

What I want to do is to sleep beside her, to hold her in my arms for hours. To stroke her hair and kiss her skin. I wonder if I'll ever feel fully sated around her. I could just watch her sleep for hours, the graceful lines of her face, the curl of her long eyelashes against her flushed cheeks. She looks so impossibly young, so incredibly beautiful. I tuck the duvet around her carefully.

She obeyed me.

For now.

My phone, which is sitting on the coffee table by the window, vibrates. I let it go to voicemail.

I know I have an unreasonable attachment, and an overblown protective instinct. The thought of her wandering, alone, on the streets, where any maniac could reach her, or speak to her, or touch her.

Or somehow steal her.

Unbearable.

My phone vibrates again. I walk over and check to see who it is.

Max.

I need to take the call but I don't want to wake her up. I'll take it in my office.

But what if she defies me, and goes out without me, even though she agreed to wait?

I won't be long.

I grab my laptop. After quietly closing the door behind me, I enter the code into the keypad to lock it.

19

I HEAR the bolt of the lock click into place.

The taste of my terror is bitter, like blood.

"I've had about enough of your sass, girl. You wait in there until I come for you. You just wait there for me and I'll show you how to respect your elders."

The room is cold, like always. It feels even colder tonight. Fear, I'm learning, is equal parts hot and cold. Your need to escape and somehow keep yourself alive no matter what...that part of it feels hot. But the rest of you feels colder than ice and so scared you think you might die.

I've seen the way he's been watching me. Some hidden instinct knows what that look means, even if I don't fully understand it.

I need to leave. Before he comes through the door he locked to do whatever it is he's promised.

"It'll be our little secret."

I'm trapped.

Outside my bedroom window, it's snowing. It's dark. Late. But there's only one thing to do.

My mother won't hear the creak of the door. She's dead to the world by this time of night, cradling her empty bottle.

No one will stop him. No one will hear my pleas, I know this. So I put on all the clothes I can, my boots, my hat, my only jacket. I pack a small bag with a wool blanket, some spare clothes and my stuffed bear. I open the window and let myself out, not bothering to close it behind me.

I know it's four miles to school and four and a half to the library, but both will be closed at this time of night. So I go to the neighbor's barn, slide through the crack of a broken board and sneak inside. It's dark and spooky, but at least it's warm. A horse neighs quietly. It gives me comfort to have him close by, and there are others. At least I'm not completely alone. I climb a ladder into the loft and pray that the farmer won't find me or somehow sense that I've broken in. There's a small pile of hay. I lay my blanket over me. I listen to the sounds of the horses below me. I think about what he'll do when he finds me gone.

Will my mother miss me? Will I ever go home again?

I cry as the prickly hay pokes me. I'm ten years old. And here in this lonely barn, I make a decision: no one will trap me or threaten me again.

"You'll like it, you'll see. No one ever needs to know except you and me."

That was when he closed the door and slid the lock into place.

I WAKE WITH A JOLT, groggy and disoriented. It takes me a few seconds to figure out where I am. *I'm not at home in the tiny rundown shack, or in the barn where I stayed for months at a time. Or the chicken coop. Or under the bridge. Or in the train station, where I was almost stolen by a commuter who was anything but.* I learned how to hide, and I learned how to run.

But that had all been a long time ago.

Reality fades in. I'm in L.A., in Rafe's plush penthouse apartment.

"Rafe?" My voice sounds weird. Edged with panic. It's been more than four years since I had a dream like that, since before I got into Stanford. I wonder why those deeply-buried traumas I'd tried to banish from my mind would come raging back now.

I call out to Rafe again but there's no answer. His computer is gone and so is he. I'm annoyed by this but it's understandable, I guess. I fell asleep. He didn't want to bother me. That's just him being considerate. Nothing more or less or anything to worry about. He promised he'd try. He left me to sleep, then he probably expects me to join him when I'm ready.

I go to Rafe's enormous bathroom and take a shower. It feels good, like some of the horrible memories are being washed away.

I dry myself with one of Rafe's oversized towels, then I put on another one of the dresses he bought me. It's a thin blue knit and tight-fitting. *Beautiful*, he said that day on Rodeo Drive. For some reason, even though it's not cold, I grab my suede jacket.

Why would I do that?

I'm just going to his office.

The dream. I'd put on my jacket that night and I'm doing it now.

God.

Maybe I need therapy. I feel surprisingly shaken by those old, awful memories. Why now?

I slide my boots on and grab my new phone. I touch my finger to the screen as I pick it up and his message is still there.

XOXO I LOVE YOU

The words make me feel better. I'm safe now. Everything's okay. Those scary, long-ago memories are exactly where they belong. In the past.

I walk over to the door of Rafe's bedroom and turn the handle.

Weirdly, it won't budge.

I try again.

My heart skips a beat as the cold terror bubbles up. I try again, twisting frantically.

No.

He locked me in.

20

I THINK I actually black out for a minute, from the shock of re-living that long-buried fear. I'm surprised by just *how* intense it is. I should be over it by now. But *that noise of the lock clicking into place.* It must have triggered some forgotten emotion. And it's the one thing I hate more than anything else: the feeling of being locked in with no escape.

I have to get out. Just like I have before, more than once.

Damn you, Rafe. How could you have done that?

We'd had that intense conversation, that night on his yacht, but I hadn't told him all the gory details of that nightmarish long-ago night. Rafe couldn't have known. Still, who locks people in? I don't care how much of a big shot he might be or how used to being in charge he is. It's completely unacceptable. This isn't a door to the outside world. This is his *bedroom*.

This isn't about protection.

It's about ownership. And control.

I don't want to be owned. Sure, I want to be loved, and cherished, what's wrong with that? But I can't do it if I'm going to lose myself in the process.

I just can't.

And he should be asking me to, it's as simple as that.

I'm too freaked out to cry, but I feel like crying. Because the best thing that's ever happened to me is now over.

I think about calling him to tell him that, but I'm too furious. He's the last person in the world I want to talk to right now. I don't care what his reasons are. This is beyond the scope of what I can tolerate.

I pick up the intercom that buzzes Rafe's kitchen. I know Rafe will be in his office. But he'd mentioned that Bennett, his chef, is working today. I notice now that there's some food on the table. I feel too sick to eat. And too devastated. "Hello?" I say into the speaker.

Nothing. The anxiety is surging through my veins like ice-fire.

"Hello? Bennett, are you there?"

A crackle. Then a voice. "Hello?" He seems surprised. Of course he would have expected Rafe's orders, not mine.

"Bennett, it's Lexi. Rafe's...girlfriend." Ex-girlfriend,

more precisely. I almost scream at him, *Let me out! Please help me!* I fumble instead with a request that might sound more reasonable. I don't want him calling Rafe. "I wondered if you could please bring me something to drink. Rafe said I could order anything I wanted, and, if you don't mind, I'd love a…bottle of champagne. We're celebrating."

"Of course," Bennett says. "Should I see if there's anything Rafe—"

"*No.*" My answer is too sharp-sounding. So I make a point of trying to tone it down a notch. "No. He's working. He won't be long. I'd like to surprise him with some champagne, if it's no trouble."

"Of course, Miss Lexi. He always keep champagne. I'll bring it right up."

"Thank you. Oh, and you'll need the code for the door if you have it. The door seems to be locked."

He pauses at this, then gives a stilted, "Of course. I know the code."

Thank God.

I can only hope he'll come right away without calling Rafe. He probably knows Rafe doesn't like being interrupted when he's in his office. This detail might be my salvation.

Another wave of panic rolls over me. I feel like I'm going to be sick. My heart is racing. I will myself to calm down. *There's no need to overreact, Lexi. You're not a child anymore and you're not being stalked by a predator. Bennett will be here in a few minutes and he'll let you out.*

But my psyche doesn't seem to want to listen. It's too deep, this fear. It goes too far back. The room feels like it's shrinking. The walls are closing in.

I hear four soft beeping sounds, then the lock clicks open.

The relief I feel when that door swings open is indescribable.

I almost throw my arms around Bennett in a fit of gratitude. Bennett is tall and strong-looking. Of course Rafe would choose someone who looks like he could bench press The Rock as his chef. You never know when some unforeseen threat might be lurking in the pantry.

He looks surprised at the state of me, wearing my luxurious coat. Or maybe it's the wild look in my eyes. I can practically see the thoughts playing across his face. *Should I have unlocked this door? Was it locked for a reason? Will I get fired and lose my ridiculously fat salary considering all I do is occasionally cook for a filthy rich mogul with questionable scruples and an imprisoned, crazed sex slave?* Or something like that.

Bennett places the silver bucket that holds the ice and champagne and two glasses on the table just outside Rafe's bedroom door.

"Thank you," I say. Then, "*Please*...please don't call Rafe." I try to tone it down in case he gets suspicious. "As I said, I want to surprise him. Besides, you know what he's like when he's working." Which sounds weird. Does he? Probably. "Thank you, Bennett," I add because this is getting awkward.

He smiles uneasily, then he walks away.

I stand in the doorway, watching him go, making sure the door stays open. I pour myself a glass of champagne, all the way to the top. Then I drink it.

I take my brand new phone and I place it on top of the almost-empty glass. I've left my other phone behind. I don't want him calling me. Or tracking me. I know for a fact he'll try to do both.

I walk through Rafe's apartment. I get the elevator down to the lobby, walk through it without so much as a backward glance, and make my way out on to the street.

21

IT FEELS strange to be back on the streets again, alone. It's now been more than two weeks since I've been away from Rafe…at all. The streets seem dirtier than I remember them, and more chaotic. I've gotten used to luxury, to an almost complete removal from the real world.

I'm also not used to the attention. People notice me, and I'm not sure why. Sure, I'm dressed in expensive clothing. My coat and my boots are both to die for. These are the details the women notice. But I'm hardly the only person on the streets of L.A. wearing expensive footwear and a nice outfit. Even so, their eyes follow me as I walk past.

Maybe that's just the way it is when you don't intentionally dress to hide yourself. When you make an effort to actually be seen, maybe you are. This is something I don't have a lot of experience with outside of Rafe's cocoon.

It's warm—not surprisingly, it's L.A.—so I leave my coat open, wishing now that I hadn't bothered wearing it. Between my panic attack and my hasty escape, I feel flushed, and spooked.

A man stops in his tracks to watch me walk past him and this unnerves me.

What the hell?

I keep walking, wishing desperately for my old sweatshirt, my coke bottle glasses and my baggy jeans. My cloak of invisibility.

Maybe my hair's a mess. I hadn't actually brushed it in my rush to get out of Rafe's apartment and hadn't put on make-up or even looked in the mirror. I glance in a window as I walk past it to check out my own reflection. Slightly wild-looking but nothing too outlandish. I smooth my hair with my hands, remembering only now that I don't even have my money card with me. *Shit.* Or anything else.

Lexi, you idiot.

But I let myself off the hook this time. I was upset, and for good reason. Now that the adrenaline is wearing off and I'm starting to fully grasp what I've just done and why, a tidal wave of emotion is waiting to break. I hold it back. I don't want to fall apart out here on the street.

Rafe, how could you do that?

I've left him.

I've lost him.

Beautiful Rafe.

Beautiful, bossy, asshole *Rafe. Who locked you up.*

Because he loves me. Because he wanted to protect me.

There are better ways to protect you. Ways that don't involve imprisoning *you.*

Yes. A line had been crossed.

What will he do when he finds me gone?

Go completely ballistic.

I decide to go into the next bar or restaurant I see and ask if I can use their phone. To call Tess. I'll get her to come pick me up. Why didn't I think to bring my bag? I'd been in such a state that I'd bolted without it.

I suddenly feel outrageously tired. What I feel like doing is going to bed, curling myself up into a ball and staying there for a week. I feel like hiding from the world, and especially him.

I can't go to Tess's. That'll be the first place he'll look for me.

I *want* him to worry about me.

I feel reckless. And utterly lost. Free, in the loosest sense of the word. Not *good* free, but loose, like I'm lost at sea or something.

"Wow," someone says, diverting my attention. I'm still looking at my own reflection and I see someone standing next to me. A man.

I glance over at him. He's tall with brown hair and dark eyes. He's wearing a business suit. A nice one. Expensive.

He's not particularly handsome but he's well groomed. He's making the most of what he has. "My name's Joe. Joe Grayson."

"Hi." Just to be polite. But I don't want to talk to Joe Grayson, or anyone else. I start walking.

Joe Grayson walks alongside me. "Can I buy you a drink? Or something to eat? I was just headed to the Italian restaurant on the corner, and I'd love to buy you some lunch." It's not a good idea. I'm in no mood to make small talk with a stranger. But the fact is, I need to find a phone and I also want to get off the street. I'm not that far from Rafe's, and as soon as he discovers I'm gone, he'll be looking for me.

"Uh...sure," I say. At least I'll be able to call Tess and tell her not to worry.

"What's your name?" he says.

"Lexi."

Joe Grayson smiles. "Nice to meet you, Lexi." He seems harmless enough, and mild-mannered. Then again, I'm used to Rafe and his passion and hot-bloodedness. Maybe my parameters are skewed at this point. Maybe *everyone* seems harmless and mild-mannered compared to Rafe.

I walk into the restaurant with Joe Grayson. It's modern-looking with lots of shiny glass. Joe offers to take my coat and hangs it on a nearby hook. His jaw actually drops when he sees my clinging mini-dress, but he catches himself. *You're a goddess*, Rafe had said when I tried it on. *I can't believe you're real. And you're mine.*

A waitress leads us a table, fills water glasses, gives us menus and takes our drink orders.

I order a glass of champagne, because why not, and Joe Grayson asks the waitress to bring us a bottle.

"So," says Joe, "what do you do, Lexi?"

The very last thing I want to do is give this stranger even the most banal details about me or my life. So I avoid the question. "Joe, I accidentally left my phone at home. Would you mind if I used yours to make a quick phone call?"

He hesitates, but then he takes his phone out of his pocket, unlocks the passcode and hands it to me.

I wonder if Rafe knows I'm gone yet.

Deciding not to bring even more attention to myself and my regrettably very-short, very-tight dress, I don't bother leaving the table. I dial Tess's number.

"Hello?"

"Tess, it's me."

"Lexi?"

"Listen, I need you to come get me. I don't have my phone or my wallet—"

"Where's Rafe? Are you okay, Lex?"

Damn it. I've been trying to keep my emotions on hold, but just hearing her concern makes my eyes start to sting. "Can you come get me?"

"Are you at Downtown?"

"I'm in a restaurant, just down the street from the offices. Tess, if Rafe calls you, I need you to tell him you don't know where I am, okay? Please. I'll explain everything when you get here."

"Oh my god, did you guys break up?"

"Yes. I guess so. I left."

"What happened?"

"I can't talk now. When do you think you can get here?"

"I'm in Anaheim in a lunch meeting with a client. I can cancel it—"

"No, don't cancel it." She needs her clients. I don't want to cost her money. I've basically ditched her for two weeks and here she is, ready to drop everything to come and save me, like the true friend she is. I feel terrible, for getting so swept away by Rafe that I haven't had time for her.

"Are you sure, Lex?"

"Yes."

"Okay. Is, like, two hours okay? It might even be just a little longer than that, but I'll be there as soon as I can."

"That's fine." What will I do for two hours?

"Have a couple drinks and something to eat and put them on a tab. I'll pay for it when I get there. See you soon, okay? Bye, sweetie." She ends the call and I hand the phone back to Joe.

He's watching me and I take a long sip of my champagne, feeling uncomfortable under his scrutiny.

I think about Rafe. I picture him going to his bedroom, finding it empty. I can admit there's a tiny shred of satisfaction knowing he'll be frantic—actually, more like *crazed*—when he finds me missing. I feel guilty about this, but, more than that...sad.

My thoughts feel muddled and hazed by the effects of the crazy torrent of emotion mixed with alcohol. I shouldn't be drinking more than I already have, but it takes the edge off my sorrow, and Joe keeps topping up my glass. He's been talking to me. I've listened enough to barely follow and sort of nod along, but my thoughts are a million miles—or more precisely, *one* mile—away from this totally one-sided conversation.

"Here, Lexi, have the last of it. I can order another bottle if you want."

Shit. We've drunk most of an entire bottle of champagne. Plus I had that glass at Rafe's.

Joe is sitting close to me in the retro-style booth. So close, in fact, that his thigh is touching mine. I try to adjust my dress, to pull it down my thighs, but it's no use. "Lishen, Joe," I start to explain, and I'm surprised to hear that my words sound slurred. I make an effort to steady myself. "Thanks for the champagne. I need to go meet my friend now." I try to stand up but the room tilts, and I sit back down.

Joe's hand slides over my thigh, and the expression in his eyes has changed. Like a shadow has drifted across his face. I recognize that shadow. I learned how to recognize it a long time ago. I know what it means. *Danger.*

"Don't go yet, sweetheart. We're just getting started. Have another drink." He slings his arm around my shoulders and his gaze drops to my breasts. This damn dress is absurdly low-cut. I clearly wasn't in my right mind when I chose it. I thought I was going to Rafe's office in it, not out on the town. Alone. "Fuck, you're gorgeous. We could get a cab back to my place. Come on, let me take you home."

Shit. This is not good.

Joe has also been drinking. Whiskey. Who drinks whiskey at lunch? But then, who drinks most of an entire bottle of champagne at lunch, either?

Joe's hands are getting bolder and his manner has changed. He no longer looks friendly. He looks focused. And very, very determined.

Rafe. I need you. I wish you were here. I wish you could have trusted me.

"Sure," I say, a clawing sense of self-preservation kicking in. Joe's phone is still sitting on the table. 13:51. Tess won't be here for another hour, at least. "Let me use the ladies' room first, then we'll grab a ride."

Grasping for self-control, I stand up. I sway slightly but manage to get my bearings enough to walk toward the bathroom. Finding it, I glance behind me. I'm relieved to see that the bathroom door, as well as the door of the restaurant kitchen, are hidden from view of Joe's table. I walk through the kitchen door. The room is hectically busy, crowded with restaurant staff. Some glance at me, but they're too busy to take much notice. I walk through, finding a service entrance, which leads out to a back alley. Weirdly, it's raining. In L.A. It's a hot, humid rain and the streets seem slick with oil. I almost turn back when I realize I forgot my coat. But of course that would be too obvious. I can't go back for it. Anyway, it reminds me of *him*. It's better this way.

Unsteadily, I make my way down the alley, taking the opposite direction from the way I came. The rain is falling steadily now. I turn another corner, walking down a side street, finding a hidden step to sit on that has an awning over it. I'll wait until it's time for Tess to come. Then I'll walk back.

Am I losing my mind? Am I deliberately putting myself in harm's way to get back at Rafe? What kind of revenge is that? Hurting myself to hurt him? What kind of idiot puts on a dress like this then goes out and gets inebriated with some shady stranger?

My throat feels tight. I feel the warm slide of tears on my cheeks. I hardly ever cry. It never seems to help. But for some reason, right now I can't stop myself. I sit on that step and sob like my heart is breaking. And maybe it is. I cry for my broken childhood and the fear that hounded me all the way through it. The desperation. The loneliness. And I cry because I found love. The real thing, even if it couldn't last.

I cry because I'm so *mad* at him. And because I miss him so much it hurts.

I try to get a grip. I wipe away my tears with my fingers. I don't know what time it is and I don't want to miss Tess, even though I'm pretty sure it'll still be a while yet. And it's absolutely pouring. I start walking back toward the restaurant. I'll inconspicuously wait across the street in a store or something until I see Tess's car.

But then I see him.

It's that man, Joe Grayson. He's waiting for me, looking out the window. He's not looking in my direction. I duck into the nearest door. It's a bar. A sports bar, dimly lit, with big screens showing a football game. It's crowded, mainly with men, I can't help but notice.

God, I'm so *drunk*. I feel light-headed. Dizzy.

I sit on the only empty stool, at the back end of the bar, hoping to be as inconspicuous as possible, but people are staring at me. I must look like a total mess. I'm wasted, soaked from the rain, I've just had the worst crying jag this decade, and my soaked, minuscule dress is clinging to me in all the wrong places.

The bartender walks over to me. He's old, maybe sixty. "What can I get you, sweetheart?"

"I don't have any money. I just need to sit here for a second."

"Sit there as long as you like, honey." He shuffles over to the end of the bar and pours a cup of coffee. Then he adds a shot of whiskey to it and walks back to place it in front of me. "This one's on the house."

I take a sip. I shouldn't drink it. It's strong but it tastes good. It starts to warm me up a little.

I'm in a dark corner and I lean my shoulder against the wall. I'm so *tired*. I don't remember ever feeling this tired in my life. I almost feel like I might pass out. I lean my head against the wall and close my eyes.

Someone's hand touches my shoulder and I open my eyes.

At first I think I must be dreaming.

Is it...no.

The room is spinning.

"Lexi, what—" He takes in the state of me. The ridiculous cling of my dress. He looks big and built and...tough. He's wearing a leather jacket and I can see one of his tattoos under the collar of his shirt. His dark hair is longer than Rafe's and his eyes are a shade lighter, more of a royal blue than violet. But just as intense. "What the hell are you doing here?"

It's Max.

22

I TRY TO FOCUS.

God, he looks so much like Rafe.

His presence is just as forceful and all-encompassing, but in a different way. Rafe's intensity is disciplined, masked by a cool awareness. Max's is wilder and closer to the surface.

A few of his friends laugh and call to him, throwing out lewd comments, but he shuts them out, focusing his undivided attention onto me.

He seems wary, of everything around us. Like Rafe always is...or was. Protective in sort of an over-zealous way.

I understand this. Maybe that's what childhood traumas do to a person and the people who care about them (if you're lucky enough to have any), who know about the layer-upon-layer damage. You get suspicious.

You're always on the lookout for the next threat. You end up morphing into a hyper-vigilant mess of paranoia.

I don't know how much Rafe has told his brother about our relationship. I cringe a little at the thought of the last time I saw Max, but I'm too dazed to worry about it. Either way, Max seems dedicated to his new mission: making sure his brother's clearly-inebriated, rain-soaked "assistant" is well cared for. He's staring at me sort of sternly.

Max looks bigger than I remember him. If I didn't know him—not that I really do—I might think he was dangerous. His black leather jacket is well-worn and adds to his bad-boy vibe, along with his tattoos and muscles. Rafe said he's a loose cannon. *He uses women. He lacks remorse. He's got a real dark side. He doesn't think of consequences. And he's still a hell-raiser.*

All of those qualities are very pronounced tonight. He is, like his brother, a stunning-looking man. His eyes are shadowed with that bruised vulnerability I recognize. He's got the same pirate vibe as Rafe. You get the feeling, though, that he'd cross boundaries Rafe wouldn't. I remember then that Max has killed a man. When he was eleven years old he killed his uncle with a knife. I feel for him, because I know what it's like to be pursued by someone big and scary and predatory. I ran; Max fought back. I understand why he would have done it.

His eyes are sparked with a moody unpredictability. In his world, this glimmer promises, rules don't apply.

Max pulls up a bar stool and sits down next to me, his eyes taking in every detail of my clearly-distressed state of mind and my outfit.

Max's resemblance to his brother is affecting me like a physical longing. My anger is being overpowered by a creeping despair. My buzz is taking on a harsh, darkening edge. I have nowhere to go, aside from one gilded cage or my best friend's couch, which is the very first place he'll look. Besides, I'm not the same person I was two weeks ago. I've had a long, lingering taste of perfection and now nothing can or will ever compare to that and it pisses me off. Damn him! The realization that I've not only been changed by him but also ruined for anything less makes me feel weirdly furious. At him. Damn that arrogant jerk for giving me the best of the best, for infiltrating me with all his goddamn glory so that anything in his wake will seem inferior in every possibly way! How will I live, knowing he's out there, walking around with his black hair and his wide shoulders and his brutal, masculine beauty?

"Lexi, what are you doing here?" Max repeats. "Does Rafe—"

"*No.* You can't tell him I'm here, Max. Please."

My desperation gets Max's full attention. Not that I didn't already have it, but this complicates things. I realize my fingers have curled around his wrist as I beg him. His eyebrows furrow with contemplative confusion.

Of course Max wouldn't know about any of this. Of

course his loyalties to his brother are much more entrenched than any of my pleas could ever be.

I draw my hand away, colder than I can ever remember being.

Max notices. He shrugs out of his leather jacket and drapes it around my shoulders. It's a gentle gesture and one I'm not expecting. It's so warm, and it smells faintly of cologne, smoke and dark masculinity. I'm not afraid of him, but there's an energy to him that kicks up the distinct feeling that I need to be careful. Max rewrites rules and so do I. Tonight, I'm not myself. I'm out of control. He seems to read this in me and on some level tune into it, and soothe it. Like we're on some kind of fucked-up wild-child wavelength.

"Tell me what happened," he says. "Tell me what you're doing here."

I'm grateful, that he doesn't immediately pick up his phone and call Rafe, that he would respect my wishes like that, even though he probably knows as well as I do that his brother might be going insane with worry and rage right about now. But Max doesn't move, or do anything at all, except wait for me to answer his question with a kind of tender patience that's somehow exactly what I need in this moment.

I don't reply right away, and Max continues, his voice calm, like he's talked people off ledges before and has a knack for it. "I just saw him, an hour or two ago. We had a meeting in his office. He said you were sleeping."

"I was."

"He said you look like an angel when you sleep."

My throat feels tight and achy when Max says that. I wish I could go back to Rafe's bed and pick up where we left off. I'd be more patient with him this time. I'd tell him I'll wait for him. I'd tell him not to lock the door.

"And then you woke up," Max continues slowly. "And at some point between then and now, something happened. Something that pissed you off or freaked you out."

Maybe because I know enough about Max's past to feel like he might almost be able to relate to my pathetic back-story, I answer him with an honesty that surprises me. "It was more about something that happened a long time ago. A memory came back to me and I...I just needed to leave."

He's watching my face, and his understanding is shock-ingly connective.

"Did my brother do something to hurt you, Lexi? Because if he did, I can assure you that he didn't mean to. He can be an overbearing asshole, that's fucking true as hell. But I can tell you this much. I have never, ever seen Rafe so affected by a woman as he is with you. I mean it. He's head over heels. Completely bonkers. And I can guarantee that he would never do anything to delib-erately push you away. His protectiveness gets the better of him sometimes. It just does. But he's basically a good guy. You should tell him what he did wrong. Explain it to him. Make him understand whatever it was he did to piss you off. I'm sure he'd do anything—and I mean *anything*—to get you back. You should give him another chance."

I'm not sure why, but I'm amazed that Max is basically trying to apologize for his brother's behavior. Max might be a deviant and a rule-breaker but he's loyal. And something in the depths of his dark, glinting eyes makes me want to trust him, and to follow his advice. Because I can see that he *gets* this part of me that no one else does. This broken, damaged corner of my soul is easy for him to detect because he's suffered, too. The only thing that saved him was the staunch and manic protection of the very person I've spent the past few hours desperately trying to avoid.

Max's words make me remember why Rafe is so obsessively protective. He *had* to be. It was the only way he could keep his little brother safe from the monsters under the bed and the predators outside the door. And even that hadn't been enough.

Rafe hadn't been trying to lock me in, *he'd been trying lock the threats out.*

If I hadn't drunk so much, I might not have said it out loud. "He saved you," I whisper.

Max is looking into my eyes intensely. "He's saved me

more times than I can fucking count. And he'll save you, too, if you let him. Let me call him."

"*No*," I say, the panic resurfacing. "Not yet," I hear myself add. I need more time. The refreshed memories are still gripping into me. But they're fading by a degree. Max's presence is helping. I can feel my logic and my love seeping into me like warmth.

Eventually, I'll go to Rafe. Maybe. I'll tell him what scares me, until he understands. Maybe, in time, I'll be able to forgive him. "He loves you," Max says.

God, I know that. Rafe scared me, but he'd only been acting on his *own* deep memories, repeating behaviors that were as entrenched as my reaction. I love him and I miss him. The past few hours away from him have been the loneliest I can remember.

But I'm not ready. I don't know if I'll ever be ready. The mess of my past clings to me as tightly and wetly as my skimpy dress.

"My apartment's right across the street," Max says. "We'll go over there, you can get those wet clothes off and we'll get you dried off and warmed up, then we'll call Rafe. Okay?"

I'm not sure it's a good idea. Some tiny voice in the back of my psyche warns me against being alone with Max Black. My brain is too muddled to analyze it. The only thing I can comprehend is how tired I am. Whatever the grandfatherly bartender gave me is only making it worse.

My head is spinning and my grip on consciousness is beginning to slip.

"I don't want to see him yet, Max. I just need to think."

"I'm not going to call him until you let me, Lexi, even though he'd want me to."

"I just need to sleep for a while. Then I'll decide what to do."

"All right. It's your call."

"Thank you, Max." I stand up unsteadily, holding onto the edge of the bar for support. I slide Max's jacket off and hand it back to him. I need to find Tess. Is it time? "I have to go."

But I'm silenced by Max's expression.

I forgot how inappropriate my dress is until Max's eyes widen. The punished, rained-on, very-thin knit fabric of my dress has stretched slightly in some places and tightened in others, and is practically see-through. My breasts are spilling out and the hem has ridden up to the tops of my thighs. My long hair hangs in damp ropes and does more to cover my nipples than the dress, but not enough.

Max hastily wraps his jacket back around me. "*Jesus Christ*, Lexi. You can't walk around like that. Rafe would torture me slowly before throttling me with both hands— and he has a fucking strong grip—if I did anything but take you home immediately."

"But I need to—" Tess. I just need to find Tess.

People are all around us. Max has slung his arm

around me and is leading me through the crowd, which seems closer now, and more attentive. My vision feels swirly and unhinged but I can hear vaguely that there are men all around us. Saying things. Rude things. Aggressive things.

"*Let* me *warm her up.*"

"*She's a little young for you, isn't she, Max? Is she even legal?*"

"*Where you goin', man? It's still early. Let her stay for a while.*"

There are others. They're messily drunk and their laughter is loose and edged with a meanness that's scaring me.

"Think of my well-being, Lexi," Max is murmuring as he half-carries me toward the door. "If Rafe hears about this and realizes I let you walk away...well, there'll be hellfire to pay. He'll beat me to a bloody pulp and I don't really want to be on the receiving end of all that, so if you don't mind obliging me on this one little detail, I'd really appreciate it."

Max swerves to shield me as his shoulder pushes against a man that's blocking our escape. A big man, with a tight t-shirt that showcases a b-grade tattoo and the hours he's spent at some sweaty gym.

"Fuck off and back off, asshole," Max says. "We're coming through so get the fuck out of my way."

This is dangerous, I realize. *What would have happened if Max hadn't found me?*

I'm suddenly immensely thankful that Max is a well-built, roughed-up renegade.

We're out on the street. His arm is still slung around me, supporting me. If it wasn't, I think I might fall. He's looking down at me and I notice again how much he looks like his brother. "You all right?" he says softly.

I'm about reassure him, but I can't. I'm too tired. The world is spinning, and it's getting faster. Max seems to understand this and he picks me up just as my balance fails me. I want to ask him to help me find Tess but the daylight is closing in on me, swallowed up by darkness. It's sudden and total and as it takes me, all I can feel is relief.

23

RAFE

THE MEETING WENT WELL ENOUGH. I made a few calls that should keep the authorities from Max's door at least for a while. The insider trading taking place from within his company is more widespread than I first thought. I'm not entirely convinced Max himself is squeaky clean, but I've given him the benefit of the doubt. As always. He hasn't told me either way whether he's actively involved or just turning a blind eye, and I haven't asked. I don't like the idea of placating people with hush money, but I'll do whatever needs to be done.

I do wish Max would fucking wise up. His recklessness could turn out to be very expensive. I told him that and he left in a mood. Said he was going to meet up with some friends at a bar to watch a game and that he'd see me tomorrow.

Until then, I have plans of my own. Plans that involve

the naked, nubile nymphet in my bed who, by this time, should be well rested.

I ordered the Tiffany ring yesterday. Told them I wanted the biggest diamond they had. I'll wait a little longer to pop the question, even though I'd marry her today if I thought she'd agree to it. Which I don't. We've known each other for two weeks and I get the feeling she'll think it's too soon. So I'll wait until she's ready. Until she doesn't feel rushed. I'll do whatever it takes to convince her that I'm the one. The only one, until the end of time.

She was mad at me this morning, cooing little complaints about the fact that she isn't queen of my empire yet. The thing is, I *want* to hire her. The few times we've discussed business in any detail, she's brought up some interesting ideas I know I could use. Behind all those plush, perfect curves and those irresistible lips is a bright, educated mind. And a sweetness that blows my head off. I really don't think I've ever met anyone who's so entirely devoid of malice or greed. Sure, she has her moments of feminine contrariness like every woman is entitled to, but underneath the stubbornness, Lexi is a shining beauty, inside and out, who just about brings me to my knees every time I see her.

That's my problem.

Those perfect curves and those irresistible lips—and everything else about her—could very well be my downfall. As fucking disciplined as I might be, I have no idea how I'm supposed to think straight with all that walking around my office. Trying to negotiate deals and manage staff is hard enough as it is.

Even worse, how do I concentrate when she *leaves*? When she goes to lunch meetings with lecherous editors or some horny Gen Z hotshot?

I can picture myself pacing around and moodily pining like a goddamn teenager as soon as she vacates the premises, disappearing to God knows where with God knows fucking who.

Even this morning, when she talked about going out shopping and meeting up with the friend she hasn't seen for a while...it got me all worked up. Which pisses me off to no fucking end. I don't *want* to behave this way. I know it's totally irrational and entirely overblown. I *know* I'm constantly testing the boundaries of what she can tolerate. But I can't seem to get myself to calm the fuck down.

She just seems so goddamn *vulnerable*. So utterly defenseless.

The thought of what she endured as a child is enough to practically see me hunting the redneck lunatic fucker down and wasting him. There'd been more than one, by the sounds of it, who threatened her. Her drunken mother's boyfriend. Random foster fathers. She said she'd managed to escape and run and hide before any of them were able to touch her. She was cagey about the details and of course I don't blame her for that. She doesn't want to rehash all that shit and neither do I. It's more important to focus on the present, and on our future together. She's here and she's safe now and I'll do everything I can to protect her with everything I have.

I stand for a minute on the glass-walled landing outside the door of my apartment, looking out over the view of the city. The day is overcast, with gathering dark clouds. That rare event: a rainstorm in L.A.

I take a deep breath, letting the fury in me fade out. I don't want to burst in the with a provoked temper. I'll be gentle with her, and listen to whatever grievances she has, which I have no doubt there will be plenty of. She'll be pissed off because I left her to meet with Max, even after I told her she could join me and help me work, which is the very last thing I wanted her to do today. It's not that I don't think she's capable. It's more to do with the fact that I knew I'd get the work done faster without her there. Without the distraction of her face. Her pouty lips. Her silky, gossamer hair. Not to mention other parts of her that are too damn inviting to disengage from in any way what-soever. Every time I finish with her, all I want to do is start all over again. To get deeper, and closer. Orgasms with Lexi aren't like endings, they're like the first taste of a new addiction, every fucking time. I want more, and more. And I'm sure as hell not going to get any work done if we're on the desk every five minutes. All I needed was a few hours of distance so I could concentrate. I wore her out and left her to sleep. Where she was safe and secure. Warm. Satisfied in every way I could think of.

I'll make it up to her. Anyway she wants. Anything she wants.

She can take out her kittenish wrath on me. She can bite me and hold me down. She'll be a little wild. Surly, like this morning. She can take me into her perfect body, squeezing and softly gripping me with petulant little clenches as she uses my rock-hard length to get herself off.

Fuck. Just thinking about her is too much. My cock is so hard it's once again pressed painfully against the zipper of my jeans. I can arrive with my temper in check but the hard-on is here to stay.

I open the door.

Something feels immediately wrong. The emptiness sort of echoes through my soul in a weird, drafty instinct. Nothing's out of place. Low music is playing in the kitchen. Bennett is here somewhere. But I'm not interested in what Bennett's doing.

I run into the master bedroom wing. Odd white-noise crackles somewhere behind my thoughts when I see that the bedroom door is wide open. A bottle of champagne sits on the small table outside the bedroom. Two glasses. On one, a phone has been neatly balanced.

Lexi's phone.

I know she's gone even before I step inside. But I run in and look for her anyway, in a kind of frenzy that's uncharacteristic even for me. I look in the bathroom. She took a shower and dropped the towel on the floor. Which is unusual. Lexi is tidy. She likes her things in order. Even when I told her she didn't have to worry about stuff like that, that housekeepers would clean up, she said she likes doing it. She likes trying to make order out of the chaos that is her life. That's how she put it.

Her clothes are still here, and all her other belongings. Her bag. Her keys.

Lexi's coat is gone, though. Her favorite, the one I bought her on Rodeo Drive. She'd been so thrilled with that coat. She said it was the most beautiful thing she'd ever worn. She even cried a little, a single tear drawing a line down her lightly-freckled cheek. I kissed her and told her how beautiful she was, with her golden hair long and loose, illuminated by that inner glow she always seems to radiate.

My Lexi is gone.

I have to find her.

24

RAFE

I'M manic and half-mad with worry. I lose all sense of control.

My brain fizzes with panic, with a sort of hyper-alert commitment, and most of all, with acute desperation. She's out there, all alone. She'll attract all kinds of unwanted attention, looking like she does. Just *being* like she *is*.

Fucking hell.

Get a grip, Rafe.

No! There's no grip! No grip at all!

I touch my fingers to a few pieces of her clothing like a pathetic wretch. What's she wearing? Is she warm enough? Is her hair still wet from her shower? She drank some of the champagne. She might be a little tipsy. Her defenses will be down.

And she's upset, about whatever it is I've done. What *have* I done, that's so fucking terrible she had to run away?

Go into my office for a while? She *knows* there's stuff that needs to be dealt with. I *told* her she could keep her job. I gave her every assurance she asked for.

I'm going to lose my shit completely if I don't find my girl.

That's all I want to do, just *find* her.

Before someone else does.

I run into the kitchen to find Bennett, cooking. Bennett's not only a chef, he's ex-military, and a body-guard. Even so, I don't think even Bennett could take me in a fight right now, I'm too manic. I grab the front of his shirt with my fist. "Where is she?"

He's shocked by my behavior. "Lexi?"

"Yes, *Lexi*. Have you seen her?"

"She asked for champagne. She wanted me to unlock the door." I can see in Bennett's eyes that he thinks I've wronged her, and it suddenly clicks. *I locked the door.*

For good reason! *To keep her safe.*

God, is that why she *left*?

Fuck! "Do you know where she went?" I realize I'm still holding Bennett's shirt. I let go of it.

"I thought she was in your suite," says Bennett. He doesn't even realize she left.

"She's not *in* my *fucking* suite. She's *gone*. Did she say where she was going?"

"No. I've been here the whole time, in the kitchen. I didn't hear her leave."

"You didn't think to fucking *call me*?" Even as I say it, I know I'm not only being an asshole but a complete goddamn psycho. I not only locked my girlfriend in my bedroom but now I'm going ballistic all over my cook because she isn't *still* locked up.

"She asked me not to," Bennett says. "She begged me not to."

This piece of information hits me right in the middle of my goddamn gut. Or maybe it's my heart. If I even have one. "She begged you not to call me," I repeat stupidly.

Lexi's gone and it's my fault. I've driven her away by behaving like the lunatic that I am.

I know all about triggers. I understand because my own brother carries the same scars and so do I, by association, through his memories and his vulnerabilities.

There are times when I convince myself I don't remember all the details of that night. But I do. It's etched there, devil-clear. Max has never been quite the same, and who can blame him? Things set him off. Random things evoke his anguish. We never talk about the memories but they swarm around us both, tainting everything. Trauma is like that: it colors your entire world, even when you try to paint over it. I do my best to calm Max down and mostly it works. The days got easier. But the nights can still be jagged, even now, broken by nightmares. Even now Max takes on a haunted look from time to time, when things bubble up.

And then I remember something else Lexi confessed to me. *He used to threaten me and…well, threaten to do things. It was terrifying.*

Maybe that's when it happened. Maybe he locked her up, the fucker.

You *locked her up, you fucker.*

If I only I could *find* her. *I have to find her.* To explain. To apologize for everything until she forgives me.

"Go, Rafe," says Bennett. "I'll wait here and if she turns up, I'll call you immediately."

I don't hesitate. I pull my phone out my pocket as I take the elevator down to the street. I'll keep Bennett—if he doesn't quit—and give him a raise, maybe, if I ever return to this apartment, or this company, or this life. I don't fucking care about any of it. I feel strangely, entirely numb. My rage has settled into an eerie, awful sense of desolation. I don't care about anything at all, except one thing.

Her.

I want her so badly it scares me. Here I am, a billionaire with a twenty-fucking-million dollar penthouse and a goddamn business empire. A gargantuan investment portfolio that's bullet-proof, recession-proof and practically tax exempt. Two Maseratis, three limos, a Maybach, a Ferrari, a Ducati, two Lamborghinis and a Gulfstream. A hotel in Paris, a ten-million dollar apartment in New York City, the Kauai estate, a house in Key West, a city block in Houston, a mansion in Malibu with a vineyard and a view of the ocean blah blah blah. A super-yacht and a forty-foot sail-boat christened Lucky, a word that just about breaks my fucking jaded heart at the realization of what I've let slip through my fingers.

None of it matters. I'd give it all to the first beggar on the street just for a glimpse of her. A touch of that silken hair. A kiss from those pink, candied lips. A chance to tell her I'm sorry.

I've driven her away with my obsession. It's *me* who scared her and trapped her and tightened the noose of my own obsession until she broke.

It's *me* she's trying to escape from. Going to dangerous lengths, possibly, to try to avoid me. Where would she go? Who would she run *to*? My mind whirls with the possibilities. I'll check out the friend—what was her name? Tess, or Tessa.

But Lexi is smarter than that: if she's running from me, she'll go somewhere I won't think to look. Does she have old friends or acquaintances she hasn't mentioned to me? Ex-boyfriends? My stomach curls grimly at the thought. She said she never found anyone she felt a real connection to, before me. None that she wanted to *give herself to*, as she gave herself to me.

So incredibly sweetly. So beautifully. *Oh, fuck. So irresistibly.*

I've blown it. I've fucked everything up. I have to find her. I *have* to. Or I'll lose my fucking fucked-up mind.

I could take one of the cars, parked in a locked fortress-like garage in my building. I could have walked the streets or call the police. Grease palms. Scour every inch of this crowded city. But no. I need to think of Lexi. I need to *earn* her trust by thinking of her, of what she might want me to do.

I need to get my shit together and act like the man she wants. I'm going to win her back if it's last thing I ever do. I'll take the limo. That way, if I find her—*when* I find her—I can jump out in the middle of the street if I have to.

My driver pulls up in front of my building and I give him a few addresses. A place to start.

The streets are crowded. It's late afternoon on Saturday, but it's L.A. The streets are always crowded. I pour myself a drink from the minibar, hoping it might take the edge off, and scan the crowds as the silence of the car throbs with emptiness.

Please, Lexi. Please don't disappear on me. Please let me find you.

Please.

Thank you for reading **XOXO I Love You.** I hope you enjoyed the first part of Rafe and Lexi's love story!

Below I've included a sneak peek of **XOXX I Love You More,** the exciting conclusion to the I Love You series.

I've also included Chapter One of **MAX**, a sexy standalone spin-off to the series, starring Rafe's brother. As I was writing this book, I knew Max needed his own HEA.

xoxo,

Julie

Please come join my Facebook reader group, Julie Capulet's Romantics, where I share cover reveals, insider info and we discuss all things romance!

Sign up for my newsletter to receive my free bonus content and get access to sneak peeks and exclusive giveaways!

Visit my website @ www.juliecapulet.com

Chapter One

LEXI

To set the record straight, I'm not usually the kind of person who wakes up in a total stranger's apartment, wearing a rain-soaked shred of a very-tight dress, drunk, lost, broke and as helpless as a girl can pretty much be. I've spent my entire life training myself to be an independent twenty-first century woman who's fully prepared to take the world by storm—and avoiding situations exactly like the one I'm in right now.

Things don't always turn out the way you wish they would.

I'm regaining consciousness after a record-breaking meltdown that I'm only now beginning to fully recall. And I'm starting to regret...a lot of things. One, letting myself get carried away by a hurricane of lust and a fairy tale of a love affair that promised from the very first second I saw him that it was way too good to be true. Two, possibly over-reacting by chugging at least twice as much champagne as a reasonable person ever would. Three, not bringing my phone so I could at least call my best friend Tess to come and pick me up.

As it is, I'm struggling even to open my eyes. My awareness feels overwhelmed by a thick, invisible fog.

Someone is undressing me, with warm, strong hands. Peeling my wet dress away from my cold skin.

Who?

"Lexi, you need to get these wet clothes off. You're soaked to the skin and you're cold. Hold still." I can't do anything *but* hold still. My body feels like it's made of lead. His voice sounds familiar, but I can't place it. "I'm going to put this robe on you and wrap you in my duvet. You need to get warm."

It takes a gargantuan amount of effort, but I finally do it. I manage to open my eyes enough to see who's here with me. As soon as I see his face, it all comes rushing back.

It's Max.

Max Black.

Rafe's brother.

Rafe, my intense, beautiful lover—and boss, possibly, although I can't remember how we left it. I'd gone to the job interview at his company, Downtown, and I'd literally been swept away by a rush of lust and attraction neither of us had been able to control. It had been crazy. Wild. And totally unlike me. I'd fallen for him from that very first second. You read about things like that happening to people, love at first sight and all that, but you never expect it to happen to *you*. I'd spent the past two weeks with him, at his beach estate in Kauai, surfing, falling deeply in love with him, telling him things I've never told anyone, and having sex with him practically every hour of the day and night, in his bed, on his private beach, on his super-yacht, on his jet...

But then, as soon as we arrived back in L.A., he'd proceeded to *lock me in his bedroom* before leaving me to go to his office.

It was one of those things—actually, the *one* thing—I just really can't handle. A hangover from a mess of a childhood I prefer not to think about.

I'd escaped. And I'd run from him. I remember everything now.

I left him.

I've left Rafe.

Max's hands are on my body as he peels off my skimpy outfit. Slowly. Carefully.

Am I wearing anything underneath my dress? A lacy bra and a tiny pair of La Perla panties. Rafe bought them for me, of course, as he'd bought me practically everything else I own, that day he took me shopping on Rodeo Drive.

I can't even speak. His hands are so insistent...and so *warm*.

I'm shivering. I sigh as his hands touch me, I'm not sure why. It feels good to have the cold layer taken off. I can hear his breathing, like it's heavier than normal. He's pulling the dress away from my shoulders, adjusting me so he can pull the wet fabric away from my skin...

The Obsession Begins

Get the FREE prequel to the I Love You series!

After graduation, Lexi moves to L.A. to stay with her friend Tess and begin her job search. By some miracle, she gets an interview for a dream job, at Downtown, the "It" company of the decade, as the CEO's assistant. If rumors are anything to go by, Rafe Black is not only one of the most ruthless men in the city, but also one of the hottest men on the planet. Lexi can only hope her shyness doesn't ruin her chances of landing herself the opportunity of a lifetime.

Find out how it all began...

**Get your free copy at
www.juliecapulet.com/bonuscontent**

I notice him as soon as he walks into my chic new Los Angeles restaurant. Of course I do. He's tall and built, with tattoos and a dark, pirate-king vibe. According to rumors, he's also an investment genius who happens to be a billionaire.

But this is no fairy tale. He's wearing one of those criminal cuffs on one wrist and a Rolex on the other.

Just what I don't need. A rich bad boy with rage issues. It's scary enough that one of my customers has been stalking me.

But when the stalker follows me home one night, it's Max who saves me—the gorgeous blue-eyed stranger who could be either the devil or a saint.

He's dangerous, but I've never felt so safe. He's a sinner who saves me in every possible way. He becomes my haven, my protector, my paradox.

And he's the love story I never saw coming...

Max is a spin-off from the I Love You series and is a sexy standalone story.

Part One

I've held back my rage for a long time but today I feel like pummeling someone—anyone—into next goddamn week. When I find out who screwed me over...I just hope I can control myself long enough not to kill the fucker and end up in a goddamn jail cell. Then again, getting convicted for a crime I actually *did* commit might be a whole lot more satisfying than getting burned for one I didn't.

I walk through the door of my penthouse office and shut the door. What I feel like doing is slamming it, smashing the place up and hunting down the asshole who put me in this mess. But those days are long gone. I'm not an amped-up punk anymore. I'm a level-headed overachiever with an Ivy League degree under my belt, five luxury properties to my name and a net worth of more than four hundred million dollars. I am—*was*, until earlier this afternoon—CFO of a Fortune 500 investment company and Chairman of the Goddamn Board of Directors.

I make a point of keeping my cool.

Barely.

I run a hand through my hair. I need a haircut. Hell, maybe I won't even bother. I won't be seeing the inside of a boardroom anytime soon. I stuff my $5,000 Armani jacket into one of the cardboard boxes now sitting in my office. Usually I don't show my tats at work but who gives a fuck? Today it doesn't matter. I roll up my sleeves and yank off my tie. My shirt feels too tight, possibly because I've been working out like a goddamn maniac lately. I start packing a few things from the shelves into the boxes.

My phone rings.

I almost don't answer it, but my brother's name flashes up on the screen. We have a deal: we always answer. No matter how shitty our day might've been. And today pretty much takes the cake.

Rafe launches straight into it. "Home detention's no reason to bail on me. Come out to dinner with us tonight."

"No. I'll see you tomorrow."

"Max," he says. "I'm getting *married* in two days. I need my best man there tonight to help me celebrate. Besides,

Lexi found a place that's right around the corner from your office. We're heading down there now to meet Lexi's maid of honor, Tess. You met her the other night."

I got convicted of insider trading today and my brother bailed me out on the spot. Instead of a jail sentence, I'll be serving a three-month stint of home detention. I've been fitted with an electronic bracelet which, if I happen to step outside my jurisdiction, will blow my fucking head off. Okay, maybe it won't. But it might as well. I've been ordered by the judge not to leave the three-block square where my apartment and my office are located. I can walk between the two, or drive my Ducati, or any of the other six cars or twelve motorcycles parked in my private garage. If I get caught outside the zone I'll get thrown in jail for at least three years with no possibility of parole. I've also been "asked" by the Board of Directors to take a break from my job as CFO of my brother's largest investment company.

I don't really feel like dinner but, hell, I owe him one. In fact I owe him a lot more than one. Six fucking million, to be exact. "Shit. All right," I say.

The only reason I'm agreeing to meet my brother and his fiancée is because they're about to get married. I want to see them. But I wish it could be the three of us and not a foursome with some over-eager friend who's guaranteed to drool over me all night. I'm really not in the mood.

I haven't been in the mood for a while.

"I didn't do it, by the way," I say. "And I'll deposit the six mil into your Bahamas account later tonight."

"Didn't do what?"

"Leak the info."

"What do you mean?"

"I mean someone framed me." I could have told him before but there was no point. There's zero evidence to back up my claims. A stack of emails written from my private account was presented to the court, making an airtight case against me. "Someone hacked into my account and sent the emails. I didn't give out any insider information. I'm clean as a goddamn whistle."

Rafe's silent for a couple of seconds, like he can't believe what he's hearing. "Why didn't you tell me this?"

"Because I knew I didn't stand a chance in court. And I didn't want to draw it out." I have a long list of criminal offenses. Mostly minor shit I did when I was younger. Even though I've spent the past ten years trying to make up for all that by working my ass off and heading several major companies, I have enough of a record to skew any judge's opinion of me in the wrong direction. I know what I look like to a judge: a badass. A shady delinquent with a history. The kind of guy the law has a problem with.

Rafe knows all this.

"I have a few ideas about who might've framed me," I tell him, "but there's no point naming names until I have proof."

"You should've told me," Rafe says again.

"I didn't want it to look like we were trying to cover something up. Then the whole company looks dirty. This way, it's just me."

"Jesus, Max."

When you're dealing with the kind of money we throw around on a daily basis, it's dog-eat-dog, everyone knows that. I earn ten million dollars a year working for my brother, plus commission, which is usually double my salary, and sometimes more. Everyone who works with me wants my job and they all think the only reason I'm there is because my brother owns the company. Which used to be true. Not anymore. I'm good at building companies and I'm good at making money. It took me a while to get on track in life but these days I can spot a winner from a mile away.

"Until then," I add, "I'll be taking a little hiatus from the office."

"I own the damn company, Max. If you want to stay you can stay."

"I can still advise the brokers from my home office. Don't sweat it. I need a break anyway."

"I'll fucking slam whoever did this."

"Yeah, you and me both."

"I'll call an investigator I use," Rafe says. "We'll get to the bottom of this."

Taking time out from my job doesn't worry me. Letting my brother down does. Those days are over.

His sigh is pissed-off. "At least let me buy you a drink."

"Fine, then. I'll see you in twenty." I end the call and set the phone on my desk, which is strewn with court orders and legal documents. Irate letters from clients questioning my ethics and calling for my dismissal.

I'll clear my name if it's the last thing I do. I swore a long time ago I'd never get another criminal conviction, so this one stings a lot more than I'd like to admit.

I pick up a pink envelope from my stack of mail. *Another one?* Hell, she just won't quit. I get a lot of cards and letters from women. This one is from a girl I had dinner around six months ago. Or was it longer than that? I met her at a charity function, I remember that much. I'd donated a lot of money to a charity that helps down-and-out teens get into college. I *was* a down-and-out teen once so I understand how much of a difference the help of one person can make. So they sent me a free ticket to the event and I'd ended up going. She saw me from across the room and confessed she moved the seating arrangement so she could sit next to me. This happens to me all the time so I didn't think much of it. The conversation had been almost entirely one-sided. She drank a lot and asked me back to her place. Even though she was sending all the wrong signals—overly needy, borderline stalkerish, the kind of woman who clings when it's the very last thing you want them to do—I'd taken her home.

A terrible decision, as it turned out, like so many are.

It had played out the way it always does. For me, it was unfulfilling because no emotion or genuine interest was involved at all. She'd told me it was the best sex of her life, begged me to stay, then had a dramatic meltdown when I tried to leave. I hadn't called or given her my number but she knows where I work and keeps sending me letters about how I broke her goddamn heart. I had to tell the door people to stop her from entering the building after she stormed up to my office once when I was in the middle of a meeting, crying and telling me she loves me.

After *one* night. Which is crazy.

Even so, it happens all the time. Go figure.

I'm probably the least lovable person I know. I'm broken, and unfixable.

I rip open the envelope.

Max, please call me. Please!!! I need to see you one more time. I know I'll be able to change your mind. I just want to talk to you. We're meant to be together. It's destiny, I can feel it. Please let me show you how much you mean to me. Please, Max. Call me back. All my love, Melanie.

I toss the card into the shredder.

I've tried to feel that spark. I *want* to feel that spark. The one that means you're supposed to be with someone for more than one night. Maybe even for—I don't know—a *month*, maybe. Or even a whole goddamn lifetime. People *do* that shit.

The problem is, I never feel that spark and I always end up regretting everything.

So I made a decision. Probably around six months ago. Soon after Melanie, as it turns out. I decided to take a break. It's the reason I've been pumping iron like it's going out of style. All that pent up energy has to be spent somehow.

My pent up energy is on overdrive at this point. I feel like I'm about to fucking spontaneously combust.

And I'm getting tired of being alone.

It's possibly what I deserve, after the way I've treated women. Dismissive. Disengaged. Non-committal to the extreme. They accuse me of using them, then walking away. Which is true enough.

Anyway, there's no point crying about it but I'm a lost cause as far as relationships go. I came to terms with all that a long time ago.

I leave a note for my assistants to finish packing up my stuff and have it sent to my apartment. I close up my office and grab my worn black leather jacket. I walk down to the street. It's a warm night for October. There are a lot of people strolling around.

Even women who are arm-in-arm with their boyfriends or husbands check me out as I walk past.

I don't get it.

Women love me, for some reason.

Love me.

I don't dwell on it but it's just one of those things.

I've sometimes wondered what it is about me they're so desperate to have. They seem to love my looks, for better or for worse. I'm built. I'm tall. And I have an edge, which is roughly equivalent to crack for women, fuck knows why.

They even wanted me before I had money. Now, they're practically rabid.

Maybe I have the aura of someone who can do things to them no one else will. Or take them past some pleasure threshold no one else can. Who knows. Whatever it is, they watch me. They call me and pursue me relentlessly, which, lately, I've been doing my best to avoid.

I know what all this sounds like: I'm ungrateful or I'm an arrogant prick.

Not exactly.

I catch up to Rafe and Lexi just as Lexi's friend Tess is arriving, as they're walking into the restaurant. Rafe slings his arm around me like he's happy to see me. He's always happy to see me. We have the kind of bond a lot of brothers don't have. We've been through a lot together, me and him, and we know we've got each other's backs. The truth is, he's bailed me out more times than I can count but I feel like that'll start to change.

Lexi gives me a hug. My brother's fiancée is a catch, no doubt about it. She's gorgeous and is one of the nicest people I've ever met. "Hey, sweetheart," I say as she kisses my cheek. I laugh when Rafe eyeballs me. He's got some control issues when it comes to Lexi but we're cool.

The friend, Tess, who I've met once before, does what they all do: checks me out. Stares. First at my face then my body. She moves to step forward but I read her intention and take a step back before she even notices. It's something I'm well-practiced at. I don't like to be touched.

"Thanks for venturing into my jurisdiction," I say.

"For you?" Tess blushes. "Anything."

I return the smile but I'm so not in the mood for this. My muscles are clenched for no particular reason. Possibly because I'm still wound up from getting convicted of a federal offense a few hours ago and escaping a prolonged prison sentence by the skin of my goddamn teeth and six million dollars.

"Tess, let's go sit down," Lexi says, thankfully steering Tess away. I exhale, releasing a minuscule shred of the ocean of tension and despair that hounds me.

We walk further into the restaurant. "This place is so cute," Tess says.

I guess it is. It's got a lot of exposed brick and wood and mirrors. The ceiling's been decorated with yellow fairy lights and hanging bulbs, giving the place a festive atmosphere. And it's busy. I have no doubt Rafe would've thrown plenty of money around to get us the prime table by the window.

I take off my leather jacket and slide into my seat. The hostess appears and says something about getting us drinks. The bell-like tone of her voice makes me look up.

Her hair is strawberry-blond, a warm, golden color with fiery copper highlights.

Her face is angelic. More than that. Exquisite. She's cute but also gorgeous. She radiates a sweet, dazzling glow that is quite literally lighting up the room.

I realize I'm staring.

She's waiting for me and her expression is intrigued but slightly hassled. They're busy tonight and I'm holding her up. She has other things to do besides stand here and wait for me.

But I take my time. I can't help it. I want to watch her a little more. Check out the soft, bright colors of her. The deep blue shade of her eyes and her long eyelashes that blink at me as she waits. The sprinkling of freckles across her nose reminds me of summer. The mesmerizing pinkness of her lips and her pale, clear skin is fascinating me.

I'm stunned. More than that. I'm slayed.

I want to spend some time just watching her and drinking in every detail.

This is not something that's ever happened to me before.

But I can't pull my eyes away.

She's slim but curvy in all the right places. *Damn. All the right places.* Maybe I've just gone too long without and

I'm suddenly suffering the hellish consequences of my self-imposed monk-like existence. My chest feels tight and my heart's pumping fast. She's so fucking *beautiful*. My cock—*fuck*—goes instantly rock hard.

Damn it.

Max. Calm the fuck down.

The combination of her glow and her sweet, hot, completely-unaware-of-it cuteness quite literally hits me like a ton of bricks.

I won't act on it. Of course I won't. I'm a guy who ruins people's lives. A loose cannon, they call me. A rebel who never toes the line. A guy who uses women and breaks their hearts.

She's way too pure for the likes of me.

I'd dirty her with all my darkness. I'd rain all over her glowing sunny day.

I can't help fantasizing, though, just for a minute. What would it be like? To ask her out? On a real date. I honestly don't know if I've ever been on one.

I try to picture it. A wholesome, glorious, strawberry blond, blue-eyed, spectacularly dazzling date.

Or maybe two.

Or ten.

Ten thousand.

Ten fucking million, all strung together so there's no separation between them.

Fuck.

ALSO BY JULIE CAPULET

I Love You Series

The Obsession Begins (free)

XOXO I Love You

XOXX I Love You More

Love You The Most (free)

Sexy Standalones

Max

Cowboy

McCabe Brothers Series

Hopeless Romantic

My Hero

Arrogant Player

Music City Lovers Series

Nashville Days

Nashville Nights

Nashville Dreams

Nashville Lights

Hawthorne U Series

Lovestruck

Paradise Series

Devil's Angel

Wild Hearts

New York Billionaires Series

Billionaire Boss

Billionaire Grump

Billionaire Devil

Billionaire Romantic

Standalone Rom-com

Beautiful Savages

ABOUT THE AUTHOR

Julie Capulet is an Amazon top 20 bestselling author of contemporary romance. She writes steamy he-falls-first romance with heart, heat and fairy tale HEAs. Her stories are inspired by true love and she's married to her own real life hero. When she's not writing, she's reading, traveling, walking on the beach and watching rom-coms.

www.juliecapulet.com

www.ingramcontent.com/pod-product-compliance
Lightning Source LLC
Chambersburg PA
CBHW061223310726
48971CB00007B/1924